Praise for *Believing In Horses*

"Wow! If you're looking for a book you can't put down, this is your book. You don't have to be a horse lover to be sucked into the emotional rollercoaster that Sadie's life has become. If you are a horse lover, you won't be disappointed, for we horse lovers know a good horse can help you overcome anything life dishes out."
-Lois Symanski, Society of Children's Book Writers and Illustrators, author

"An emotional story, writer Valerie Ormond takes Sadie and her tri-colored Pinto horse, Lucky, through a tale of heartbreak, suspense, determination, and love."
-Blaze Magazine for Horse Crazy Kids

"It is a great story about not dwelling on loneliness, becoming passionate about something, becoming an advocate, reaching out to others, making new friends, and helping animals - all things young readers will love! Young readers are very altruistic at heart and will really relate to the main character's persistence and this story's ultimate lesson in finding out that when you help others, you are helping yourself!"
-Terry Bosworth, Maryland Reading Teacher

"The story of Believing In Horses is one of a young girl finding her voice and the strength to fight for others while simultaneously finding those same things for herself. It's not so much a coming-of-age as it is a coming-of-self, a discovery of a central character component that likely foreshadows the woman her grandchildren will one day come to know and love."
-Coastal Style Magazine

Believing In Horses

Believing In Horses

Valerie Ormond

Printed in the United Stated of America

ISBN 978-0-9736330-2-3

Library of Congress Control Number: 2012936893

2 3 4 5 6 7 8 9 10

Dedicated to Horse Savers,
military families,
and Dad

A portion of the proceeds will be donated to
the rescue organizations mentioned in this
book.

Contents

༆1༉

NEW HOMES FOR HUMANS AND HORSES

Sadie believed that everything happens for a reason.

It kept her strong and helped her cope with what seemed to be never-ending changes in her life. At twelve years old, she had already moved six times and was now beginning her fifth school. Since she considered herself an adventurer, the moves were not tragic, but learning new routines and making new friends was getting a bit awkward as she grew older.

This move, to Bowie, Maryland, came with additional stress factors. Not only was she leaving her beloved San Diego, California, where the weather was perfect and every day was a "hang outside" day, but the whole reason for the move didn't make sense.

Sadie's father was in the Navy. She was always proud of that fact, particularly when her dad would pick her up from school, soccer practice, or riding lessons, dressed in his sharp, crisp, Navy uniform. He called her "Punkin," half the time, which he derived from "Pumpkin." To most kids her age this would probably be embarrassing, but to her it was just another part of their special bond. He had been in the Navy her entire life, and even though the Navy was the cause of the moves, she loved being part of the Navy family.

But now she and her family, which included her parents and her brother Austin, had moved across the country to Maryland, near Dad's new duty station in Washington, D.C., only to find that her dad would be deploying to Afghanistan for a whole year. She couldn't help but feel sorry for herself about the move, and that made her feel guilty because her dad would be going into harm's way. Somehow it just didn't seem fair. Why couldn't the family have stayed in California? Her mom had explained it to her in a way that probably made sense to adults, but all Sadie knew was that she left a place she loved for a place she already hated.

The move didn't come without some form of consolation. Her reward for being such a trouper was that she could get her own horse. Sadie had ridden since she was five and had fallen in love with horses well before that.

While she had tinkered with other hobbies through the years including karate, soccer, painting, playing the piano, swimming, and dancing, nothing else came close to her passion for horses. She didn't just enjoy riding horses, she loved everything about them. Grooming them, talking to them, watching them, walking them with a lead rope, feeding them – anything to do with horses, she loved. She even loved the smell of the barn, which seemed odd to some non-horse lovers but well understood by those bitten by the horse bug. To Sadie, there was no better day than one spent hanging around a barn.

The next best thing about the move was her discovery of a wonderful barn, Loftmar Stables. The most fantastic part about it, aside from excellent horse care, was that she could walk there from her house. It was practically in her backyard. In all her years as a horse enthusiast she'd never had that freedom. She loved the idea of being independent from adults who could only drive her at certain times. Sadie could also hang around after her lessons, which she currently was taking using Loftmar's horses until she bought her own. She had only ever ridden barn or lesson horses, and adored every one of them.

What a luxury it was to not hear the familiar, "It's time to GO, Sadie," when whoever was toting her to and from the barn expressed total displeasure with her total pleasure of staying at the barn as long as possible. Sadie learned so much from watching other students, boarders, blacksmiths or "farriers," and barn workers. Horse care involved many facets, and she wanted to learn them all. Her past instructors called her a "sponge," because she absorbed knowledge about horses so quickly.

Sadie adopted the philosophy of several professional horsepersons, "the learning never ends." She digested everything she could from the internet, horse forums, feed and tack stores, and her lessons. She also knew the importance of hands-on education, which she got at the barn.

Mom and Dad told Sadie she had to find a suitable boarding stable before she got her horse. Knowing that it was the biggest obstacle between Sadie and her dream horse, she moved it to the top of her "to do" list.

Even though Sadie was convinced that Loftmar

3

Stables would be the perfect home for her new horse, Mom and Dad insisted she look at other stables. She tried to argue that she would never find another stable so close. She persistently stated that Loftmar took very good care of their horses, had lessons on site, and even had trails. Though her parents agreed that Loftmar appeared to have all the right things, they still wanted Sadie to explore other options to make sure that she wasn't just making a convenient decision.

Sadie's brother, Austin, proved a great help in the stable hunt. Austin had turned sixteen in January and earned his driver's license. During their move across the country, Austin drove most of the way for practice. After hearing their parents' insistence, Austin promised to chauffeur Sadie to stables so she could check them out. The arrangement was ideal; Austin got to practice driving in his new hometown, and Sadie had the freedom to explore new stables.

Austin wasn't like most of the big brothers Sadie's friends had. He was kind, patient, giving, and never had to do anything to be cool. Fiercely loyal, he loved his little sister and his family and wasn't ashamed to show it. As far as Sadie was concerned, she had the best big brother in the world. He was different.

At six feet tall, Austin inherited the best looks from both sides of his family heritage; Irish on Mom's side and Mexican on Dad's. He had his dad's beautiful dark skin and his mom's sparkling blue eyes. His shoulders spread as wide as a barn door, and he had a body builder chest. Austin enjoyed all types of sports and exercise, running, swimming, and lifting weights. Due to his athletic build, the new schools over the years had tried to recruit him for their sports programs, but Austin preferred to work out on his own.

Because of Austin's appearance, Sadie's parents felt comfortable with the two of them looking for a barn unsupervised. Anyone would have been crazy to mess with Sadie in Austin's presence. He was not only imposing and looked far more mature than his age, but he also had a "guard dog" aura to him that even the least perceptive human could see.

Although Sadie really liked Loftmar, she didn't mind the idea of the stable hunt. Seeing a few other stables in the area seemed interesting. So, with an open mind and a list of three local stables she had selected, they set off to explore. She would have liked to say her choices were scientifically based, but they weren't. The first one, Connor's Horse Home, she picked because she liked the name. The second, Jake and Tom's Stables, was far enough away that Mom and Dad would see she was putting in effort. She picked the third, Marlboro Horse Ranch, because it sounded Western and reminded her of California.

Sadie and Austin had all day Saturday to meander through the countryside and see the stables. Sadie was the navigator and steered Austin to Connor's Horse Home. They found it fairly easily using a GPS and directions from *The Equiery*, a Maryland horse magazine. They drove down a long dirt driveway to a set of barns and several fields full of horses. After they parked, Sadie hopped out looking for someone to talk to. A high school girl in low cut jeans and a tight shirt scowled at Sadie and asked: "What are you here for?"

Sadie felt instantly irritated. "We saw your stable listed in *The Equiery*," she said, "and we're looking for a place to board our new horse."

"Who is 'we?'" asked the rude girl.

Sadie wanted to ask the girl why she was being so nasty, but decided to take the high road and answered, "My brother, Austin, and I." Just then Austin joined them. For some reason he was wearing a cowboy hat today, probably because they were visiting horse farms, and even his little sister had to admit that he looked quite handsome. The rude girl transformed in an instant, like chameleons that change color. Sadie had seen them in science.

"Well, then, let's see what we can do, darlin," Sadie almost vomited as she detected a sweet Southern accent that hadn't been there a minute ago. The girl primped her hair, and smoothed her dirty, skin-tight clothes. "Mah name is Rachel, and let me tell you a lil' bit about mah farm." She reached out to shake Austin's hand and said, "And you ahhr....?" .

Austin said politely, "I'm Austin, just like my sister said."

"Oh, why yes, of course, forgive me if Ahh was a bit distracted. It's just not every day that we get such, well, that we have such *interesting* visitors." She drew out the "interesting", probably thinking it made her sound like an adult. Sadie thought she sounded like something out of a vampire movie.

"Well, Austin, let's walk around, and Ahh can show you the stables, and the fields, and tell you about all the good reasons why you should board your wonderful horse here with us," continued Rachel. Although the girl irritated Sadie, she enjoyed seeing Austin get this kind of attention. The best part was that he was bored by it. Austin would never fall for a girl like this, especially because of the way she was treating Sadie.

Just then, an older woman, who reminded Sadie of her Grandma Collins, came up to the barn with three dogs following slowly behind. She surveyed the situation, looked directly at Sadie, and asked, "Can I help you?"

Sadie chirped, "Yes, ma'am, as I told your daughter, or granddaughter, my name is Sadie, this is my brother, Austin, and we're looking for a new home for our horse. You see, we just moved here from California, and we don't really know anyone, and..."

"That's fine, dear, I get the picture. First, let me introduce myself. I'm Mrs. Connor, and this farm has been in my family for years. I don't ride much anymore, but I still love horses. Second, Rachel is not my daughter or granddaughter; she works here at the farm. I hope she didn't mislead you otherwise. Sometimes...."

"But I didn't...," Rachel whined.

"And third," continued Mrs. Connor over Rachel's objection, "although you both seem like fine young people, we don't have room for additional horses right now. We rarely have openings. When we do, I normally post a sign out by the driveway, someone calls, and I have a new boarder within days. I can take your number if you'd like, but quite honestly, I can't guarantee that I'll remember to call the next time there is an opening."

Sadie liked Mrs. Connor's honesty. She also had to admit she enjoyed seeing Rachel looking horrified that she had been found out to be a worker rather than an owner of this lovely property. Forgetting her newfound accent, Rachel turned to Austin and said, "I'm glad Mrs. Connor came to help so I can get back to work now. I hate distractions. Bu-bye."

Austin gave a small wave and forced a crooked

smile. Mrs. Connor shrugged her shoulders and chuck-led. "And one more thing, kids, you may not be aware of this because I hear they do things differently in California, but people usually make appointments when they are going to visit boarding stables. If you are going anywhere else, you may want to call ahead. Good luck with your search, and welcome to Maryland." With that, she left, her three old dogs in tow, while Sadie thanked her for her time.

They got back into the car, and Sadie checked Connor's Horse Home off on her list and made some notes. Austin, in his usual way, did not say anything about the event. He just asked, "Where next?"

"Let's see," she said, "I think we should go to Jake and Tom's Stables next, since it's furthest away."

Sadie navigated their way to the vicinity of Jake and Tom's Stables. She had always been good with directions and maps, and prided herself on her ability to use them instead of routinely relying on a GPS. As they got closer to Jake and Tom's Stables, the neighborhood changed. It became different from the other places they'd visited in Maryland. The houses were dingy; there were broken fences and cars without wheels sitting in fields. There appeared to be a layer of soot everywhere.

The further they went, the dingier the scene became. Was it partly her imagination? Something just didn't feel right.

๛2๛

RESPONSIBLE OWNERSHIP

They suddenly found themselves at a dead end in the woods without a horse farm in sight. Sadie swore she heard a bat, but kept it to herself. It was daytime and bats don't come out during the day. She wasn't sure she actually knew what a bat sounded like either.

She pulled out the paper map and reluctantly consulted the GPS with Austin. They decided to back-track. After a few wrong turns, and an ominous "Keep Out" sign or two, they ended up on Turf Lane, the street that led to their destination. Finally, they found a small hand-painted wooden sign that read, "Jake and Tom's Stables."

Austin turned down the driveway. He looked at Sadie. "You sure you want to keep going? It doesn't look very nice." She looked straight ahead and nodded to give the okay. When Sadie had her mind set to something, she could be pretty stubborn, or so she had been told. *Besides,* she thought, *things aren't always as they may appear at first, right? Look at Mrs. Connor's farm – if I had made an opinion based that wretched Rachel, I would have been all wrong.*

They continued on. The fields were muddy and manure-filled, and looked like they hadn't seen a tractor, for months or maybe years. The fences were broken, the water troughs were filthy, and the run-in sheds were half falling down. The sheds were supposed to provide shelter from rain, wind, and sun. The sheds they saw couldn't provide shelter on a perfect day.

Each field housed at least ten horses, and they appeared to be in various forms of fitness. Some looked healthy and young, and some looked beaten and old. They all had one thing in common - they all looked sad. Sadie saw one paddock where all the horses seemed overly fat. Sadie pointed and said, "Look there, it looks like they're getting enough to eat," trying to be positive.

"They're pregnant," responded Austin. She realized he was right. She looked closer and saw that, even with their big bellies, they looked malnourished. She'd had enough of this place.

"Come on, Austin, let's go. We don't even need to talk to anyone. We can check this one off the list. Mom and Dad will understand." Stubborn Sadie conceded.

Austin nodded and turned the car around, and when he started back down the road, a big black pick-up truck appeared out of nowhere and pulled up two feet in front of them, blocking the way. A large man with greasy black hair, bushy eyebrows and an overgrown moustache sauntered out of the truck, leaned against it, and said, "Not so fast."

With only those few words, Sadie recognized the accent as something she'd only heard in movies and television shows. This wasn't a Maryland hillbilly accent, but something more like a New York street scene.

A more wiry man scampered out of the passenger side of the truck.

"Whadda yous kids doin' heah?" grunted the Big Man. Sadie and Austin both froze for a moment, and then in a panic, Sadie went to get out of the car to explain why they were there. Fortunately, Austin placed his arm across her so she couldn't move.

Now the skinny man started, "Hey, din't yous heah ma cousin? He asked whacha wuz doin' heah," and he approached so close to Austin's door that they could smell his sweaty polyester suit.

Sadie thought she heard Austin growl. She was about to answer when Austin, cool as a cucumber, said, "Sorry, we took a wrong turn. We were just leaving."

Thank goodness Austin spoke. Sadie would have prattled on about the move, her horse, the farms they were visiting, how bad this particular farm looked, and on and on.

Skinny went back to join the Big Man at the truck, and they conferred for a minute. The Big Man, probably the smarter of the two, pointed at the California license plates on the car, which to him seemed to confirm the story that they were just kids who were lost. He sent Skinny back to the blocked car to say they could go. But Skinny didn't do it without some hollering.

Austin could feel the spit on his face as the bully yelled, "Din't yous see the "Keep Out" signs? Are yas stupid?"

Sadie, though her heart was pounding, opened her mouth to say something, but got a hard pinch on her thigh from Austin. Austin answered, "Yes, I'm stupid, and I'm sorry. I'm afraid you are frightening my sister now, so can we please go?"

Skinny started to mimic Austin, and the Big Man was getting impatient. He honked the horn and hollered, "Hey Jake, get back in da truck for cryin' out loud already!" Skinny started to walk away, then turned back and kicked the car, which had to hurt his foot more than the car. He tried to walk away as if it didn't hurt but couldn't hide the limp. Sadie swore she heard Austin growl again. The two cousins turned the truck around and spun out in front of Sadie and Austin.

Wow, Sadie thought, *to think I thought Rachel was bad.* The search for her future horse's new home was not going well.

They left the driveway without saying a word. Sadie slowly stopped shaking and her heart slowed down. Austin remembered the way back out to the main road. When they figured they were safe, Austin asked Sadie, "So.... do you think we should call the next place before we go?" With that, they broke into laughter.

They both had been scared, but the laughter released some of their fear. They realized they had gotten themselves into a bad situation. The stables had been listed in the online stable directory, but there were "Keep Out" signs. Sadie really didn't want to think about it anymore and wrote a big "NO!" next to Jake and Tom's Stables.

Sadie called Marlboro Horse Ranch and reached a cheery Miss Patsy, the Ranch manager.

"Sure! Come on by," Miss Patsy said. "If nobody is at the house, look for me in the truck somewhere on the farm. I'll be doing the feed. Oh!" she continued, "And don't worry about the dogs. One of them is a Rottweiler, and the other is a full-bred Rottador, which is a Rottweiler and Labrador mix. They might look scary, but the worst Princess and Diego could do is lick you to death."

Sadie was grateful for the warning. She didn't need any more excitement for this day!

The ranch was a little further than Sadie thought it would be, but easy to find. They drove through a small town, and just at the outskirts, across the railroad tracks, was the Marlboro Horse Ranch. Sadie liked it right away, with its large green pastures, scenic pond, trail paths she could see through the trees, and lots of horses. She saw something she hadn't seen at the last two places - people visiting their horses. As they drove by, a few folks waved, and Sadie and Austin waved back as if they had been here many times.

They continued up and down a hill and around a bend until they saw a house in the distance. As they were driving towards the house, a truck pulled up in front of them, reminding them both of their recent excursion. But this time, two giant dogs leaped off the back while a blond, healthy-looking woman opened the driver's side door, jumped down, and hollered above the barking, "And you must be Sadie and Austin." Sadie stepped out and waved as the two behemoth dogs surrounded her, tails-a-wagging.

Sadie introduced herself and pointed to Austin, who was getting out of the car to shake hands. They thanked Miss Patsy for welcoming them on such short notice.

Miss Patsy looked to be a little younger than Sadie's mom and her physique suggested years of hard farm work. When she spoke, her entire face smiled. She didn't need designer clothes or make-up; she had a natural beauty that seemed to come from her heart.

"We may not be the fanciest barn in the area, but I'd say we're close to being the friendliest. Why don't you two just leave your car here and come with me in the truck to see the farm." Her voice was full of warmth. " I'll tell you a little about the place. No hard sell here, we have plenty of boarders. I like to tell people up front what we do and don't do, so there aren't any misunderstandings down the road. Honesty up front – it's worked for years."

As soon as Miss Patsy fed grain to the two horses in the field by the pick-up truck, Sadie jumped into the front and Austin got in the back seat. Even though he was bigger, Sadie would be doing most of the talking and listening. It didn't matter to Austin. This was his sister's show. He would actually have been happiest sitting in the far back with the dogs, but that probably wouldn't give Miss Patsy the best first impression of the new potential boarders.

Miss Patsy drove and pointed towards the barns at the top of the hill. If they were needed, there were enough stalls for every horse on the ranch. Usually, the horses lived as naturally as possible, spending almost all of their time outside. No more than three horses shared a field, and they all had to get along. The horses had full access to grass pastures, unlimited large round bales of hay, fresh water at all times, grain twice daily, and were sheltered in sturdy run-in sheds, each built to provide the best protection from the wind.

"We have some of the healthiest, happiest horses in Maryland here, even if some people say the horses are a little chubby," Miss Patsy beamed.

As Sadie watched the horses in the field, she could see why Miss Patsy was so proud. These horses grazed lazily, played with each other, and energetically greeted the truck as it pulled up. Miss Patsy called each horse by name and easily shooed them out of her way as she dropped their grain in their feed buckets. The horses looked strong, probably because they used their muscles roaming the pastures and chasing each other around.

"Now I'll tell you what we don't do," continued Miss Pasty, as she continued feeding. "We don't put on horse blankets or take them off. We don't hold horses for vet visits or for farrier visits. We don't provide de-worming, and we don't groom or exercise horses. We see all those as jobs horse owners should do. Also, with as many boarders as we have, we don't have the staff to provide these services at the prices we charge."

"But what happens if a horse gets hurt and the owner isn't out here?" Sadie asked, always concerned about the welfare of any horse.

"Oh honey, of course we help out in an emergency, but I just wanted to spell out very clearly that we are not one of those fancy dancy barns that does everything including riding the horse for you. You'd be surprised what people expect. I have to ask myself sometimes why people even want horses if they don't want to do anything to take care of them. There's a whole lot more to horses than the riding."

"I know, and I like everything about taking care of them, even though I've never had one of my own," Sadie said proudly. "But I do kind of worry about how I would get out here for blanketing, and vet visits, especially when it gets dark early. Even though I know that horses are more important than school, my parents don't see it that way." Miss Patsy and Austin laughed.

Sadie thought for a minute.

"Miss Patsy, are there any other kids that board horses here, so I could share those jobs if we decided to board here?"

"Well, sweetie, unfortunately not right now. Most of our boarders are adults and older folks. Even though I teach lessons to anyone who is interested, a lot of the young folks these days want to be at the barns that have equestrian teams and do lots of showing. That's just not what we do here. And my own kids have more chores than they can handle, so sharing with them wouldn't be an option."

Sadie didn't like the answer, but she really liked Miss Patsy's honesty about everything. She didn't say it out loud, but she wasn't too interested in being the only young boarder at the farm.

They completed the feed routine, and Miss Patsy pointed out the training round pen, two outdoor riding rings, and the entries to the wooded trails. Before they knew it, they were back where they started.

"And that's about it. Hope you liked it, and here's my card if you think you are interested. Either way, it was real nice meeting you two. I wish all boys were as quiet as your brother there. Don't understand why so many people with nothing to say think they have to fill the space with something." She smiled and waved as they got out of the truck, and Princess and Diego remained on their tailgate perch, tails still wagging, as if waving goodbye also.

What a relief to have had a normal visit. Sadie and Austin both liked the Marlboro Horse Ranch but realized it had a few drawbacks for their situation. It was a bit too far away, and Sadie would always need a ride. That would impact Austin. It would be tough to be out there during the day for vet and farrier visits. Blanketing would get complicated, particularly when it warmed up. It was dangerous to keep blankets on horses when it got warmer because they could easily overheat. Finally, there was no one her age here. Sadie didn't need other kids around to love horses, but she knew she would sometimes run into problems with her own horse, and wanted some other kids around to bounce ideas off of.

So, Sadie pulled out her checklist and wrote, "A possibility," next to the Marlboro Horse Ranch. Her stable hunt was done. She had been objective, and felt even more comfortable than ever about having her horse live at Loftmar. Mom and Dad had been right, investigating other options made her appreciate exactly why Loftmar was the perfect stable for her.

Her day of exploring exposed her to some things she hadn't thought about. She couldn't wait to tell Mom and Dad about their adventures, but knew she had to be careful about her description of what happened at Jake and Tom's. Actually, she wanted to forget all about that incident, although she knew it would be impossible to forget those poor horses she had seen there. Maybe someday she'd find a way to help them.

❦3❧

THE PERFECT HORSE

Sadie had looked for the perfect horse her entire life. She wasn't naive, and she knew her parents didn't have that much money. But it didn't stop her from dreaming.

She wanted a horse, a partner, a being she could live and learn with. Her "perfect" horse was not a certain color, it was not a certain size; it did not even have a certain temperament. She spent a lot of time around barns hearing about the Morgan look, or the Arabian temperament, or the Quarter Horse sensibility, but she had no favorite. To her, they were all just beautiful, incredible, lovable, huggable creatures. Now that she had settled on Loftmar Stables, she could begin her search. To say she was excited was an understatement; she could barely contain herself.

The options were overwhelming. She checked

the local newspapers, horse magazines, and the tack and feed shops, which always posted horse classified ads. She talked to people at Loftmar. She viewed the hundreds of horses available via classified ads on the internet. Sadie found there were many, many horses out there, and it would be very difficult for her to choose.

Sadie needed to set some criteria. She decided she would only look at horses, not ponies, since it seemed she was getting taller and lankier every day. She knew that people measure horses and ponies in hands, the width of a large human hand placed pinky to thumb from the ground to the highest point at the withers, just below the mane. Each hand equals about four inches, but horse people would never say a pony is "58 inches or less." They would say "14.2 hands or less." This is well under-stood in the horse world.

Sadie's horse budget was $3000, lower if possible. Sadie's dad recommended she look at horse auctions be-cause he heard they had good deals.

Sadie researched some horse auction web sites and found many different types. Some horse auctions sold high dollar expensive sport horses, some sold racing Thoroughbreds, some sold Western stock-type horses, and some sold everything under the sun.

As Sadie read through web sites, she found her-self disturbed by a few things she saw. She hadn't real-ized that people sometimes used auctions to dispose of unwanted horses. She decided to avoid auctions.

As the horse search went on, Sadie felt more and more frustrated. What she thought would be an exciting time was turning out to be no fun at all. The more she looked, the more indecisive she got. *Okay, more criteria,* she thought.

The horse should not be more than fifteen years old, because Sadie wanted to have it for a long time. So, under $3000, at least 14.3 hands high, and less than fifteen years old. That limited her choices to 512 horses in the Middle Atlantic Region area from just one web site!

She needed some help with this. Fortunately, Sadie's angel, her Grandma Collins, came to her rescue just as her stress seemed to be peaking.

Grandma Anna Collins' motto was to live life to the fullest, and she wanted Sadie's life to be even fuller than her own. The first fifty years of her life was in an era where women were not allowed to fulfill their dreams. She'd kept herself contained during those years so as not to embarrass her family. But the past twenty years had been hers, since her husband passed away, and times had changed. She was seventy-two, and living every day as if she only had a few more days left.

Grandma Collins didn't even hesitate to join the "Over-70 Surf Club" in San Diego, from the moment she first heard about it. A swimmer her entire life, she had never set foot, or body, on a surfboard and wanted to see what it was all about. Many members of the surf club had been in the same boat (or surfboard) as her. Her leadership skills landed her the role of President of the club after only one year in the organization.

The Irish are known to be full of stories, and Grandma Collins was no exception. While many people claimed to be Irish, Sadie knew that her grandmother had the real woollen thread. Sadie's mom told her that Grandma Collins was the descendant of Michael O'Rourke, who had emigrated from Ireland in 1850 during the famous Potato Famine. Grandma couldn't be any more Irish, except for the fact that she had grown up in the United States. Sadie knew her Irish story-telling Grandma was truly blessed with the luck of the Irish, which she always wanted to share with her granddaughter.

It was no wonder that Grandma Collins found the perfect horse. Back in the day, Grandma used to ride. In those days safety rules were different. Grandma usually rode bareback, and her joy in riding was feeling a horse's muscles move underneath her. To Grandma, horseback riding was easy; if you could feel the movement, you could ride. Be at one with the horse. Don't fight the horse. Let any horse know you are in charge, but let the horse have fun. Simple.

Grandma found a horse in California she thought would be perfect for Sadie. He was unique. His sire was a large bay Andalusian. His dam was a National Show Horse, a mix between an Arabian and an American Saddlebred.

Arabians are known for their intellect, fine features, and endurance, and the American Saddlebreds are known for their obedience, size, and trainability. Sadie's horse was a cross-breed, bred to combine the best characteristics to make someone a perfect horse.

A tri-color pinto, the horse had three white stockings and a sock, a half-black half-white mane, and a thick, luxurious full black tail. With the build and temperament of the Andalusian and the intelligence of the National Show Horse, this horse was very special.

Although Sadie thought every horse was beautiful, she had never truly seen perfection until she'd seen an Andalusian.

Sadie had lived in Spain as part of her dad's Navy career. When Grandma Collins came to visit, the family went to see the famous Andalusian horses at Real Escuela del Arte Ecuestre, or the Royal Andalusian Riding School in Jerez, Spain. Sadie had been young, but had never forgotten the way the Andalusians there seemed to dance. Grandma remembered Sadie's love of those horses.

Full-blooded Andalusians were well out of the Navarros' price range. This turned out to be a good thing because Grandma wouldn't have found "Sadie's horse" otherwise.

The clincher was that the horse's name was "Color Me Lucky." He was born on St. Patrick's Day, which convinced Grandma Collins that there could be no better choice for Sadie. He had just turned four, and had been saddle broken but not extensively ridden. According to Grandma, Sadie could finish training him the way she wanted, "With no one else's bad habits left behind."

Lucky stood 15.1 hands high, an excellent height for Sadie, and according to the owner and breeder, had the sweetest disposition in the world. The breeder, Amy Groen, ran a small ranch and had four children. One of her daughters, Lauren, believed that Lucky was very perceptive and intuitive, and understood what Lauren was feeling. Grandma believed Lucky would be Sadie's new best friend.

Grandma Collins talked to Sadie before sharing any of this news with her parents. She wanted Sadie's thoughts before taking it to Mr. and Mrs. Navarro. Everything sounded so right, and Sadie felt relieved that her horse search might be over. Computer savvy Grandma sent Sadie the links to the horse advertisement, the e-mail exchanges between herself and Mrs. Groen, and even a YouTube video of Lucky walking, trotting, and cantering in a round pen.

Sadie opened Lucky's classified ad, and he took her breath away. She knew he had to be the one. Kind eyes, beautiful colors, a rich full mane and tail, and perfect conformation. Sadie understood the importance of conformation, or the horse's build. She knew if the horse's back is too long, or legs too short, or shoulder not sloped enough, or hooves turned out, the horse might have difficulty doing certain movements. Not only was Lucky well put together, Sadie could tell just from the look in his eye he was smart. Boy, Grandma sure knew how to pick them!

She opened the YouTube video and watched a woman, Mrs. Groen she assumed, schooling Lucky in the round pen. Lucky moved effortlessly and responded immediately to each request. Mrs. Groen's gentle nature and natural horsemanship style appealed to Sadie and worked for Lucky. Sadie studied the playful way he moved and turned, and his expressions when watching Mrs. Groen. Her excitement grew as she imagined herself schooling this lovely animal and having him listen to her so intently.

Sadie finally read the e-mail exchanges, and she had to crack up at Grandma's e-mails. She wasn't exactly playing hard to get as the buyer.

"I MUST HAVE THIS HORSE FOR MY GRANDDAUGHTER!!!! Now, can you tell me a little more about him?" Grandma had written. Mrs. Groen explained his temperament, his breeding, his training so far, and his inquisitive nature. She wanted to keep him, but they had too many horses and not enough time so she had to let him go. She went on to say that if Grandma didn't want him, she would probably keep him, and that she was kind of sorry she had put him up for sale. Sadie read this as,

"If you don't buy him now, there won't be another chance."

Sadie decided she liked Mrs. Groen. It was obvious she cared a lot about this horse and wanted to make sure that IF she were going to sell him, he would go to a good home. She had asked Grandma questions that showed her concern for her horse's welfare. Sadie looked forward to the time when she could ask her a few questions herself. But first, she and Grandma had to find out how to tell Sadie's parents that the horse was in California.

Sadie and Grandma hatched a plan, something they had done many times over the years. Just being able to work with Grandma like this from Maryland made Sadie not miss her so much. One of the things Sadie regretted most about leaving San Diego was leaving Grandma behind.

Two kindred spirits, over sixty years apart, connected at the heart and developed a unique, close relationship. In San Diego, Sadie and Grandma spent actual time together instead of virtual time and had enjoyed each other's company for several years.

When Sadie and her family had lived in Spain, it was Grandma Collins who had talked Sadie's parents into letting Sadie go to a local elementary school off-base , one of Sadie's greatest adventures. She experienced Spanish culture first hand with her classmates and became fluent in Spanish at a young age. Unfortunately, Sadie had to repeat third grade the next year in an on-base Department of Defense school, but she wouldn't have traded attending the Spanish school for anything, except maybe a horse. "Live while you are young!" Grandma Collins always said, and so Sadie did.

Sadie begged Grandma to move with the family to Maryland, but Grandma couldn't do it. She didn't want to interfere with child raising, and she had her own busy life in San Diego. Besides, who would run the Over-70 Surf Club? Grandma said that with technology today, they would hardly be able to tell there was an entire country between them. Sadie was beginning to believe that maybe Grandma was right.

The plan went like this: when Sadie's parents came home from work, Sadie would tell them she and Grandma had something very important to discuss with them. Even though Grandma Collins was Mom's mom, Dad could talk with her better than Mom most times. Dad had a calming influence on everyone and everything, be it human or animal, and had the incredible gift of listening. Dad wasn't perfect, but he always listened. Both Mom and Dad had to be there together for this to work.

Grandma would do most of the talking. She would call, and they would discuss Sadie's horse on the speaker phone. She would accentuate all of his good qualities and mention that she found him on the internet classifieds. Grandma, who could be very persuasive, felt she would easily seal the deal with her parents when she offered to buy Lucky because she was so sure this was the right horse. Once they agreed, Grandma would mention Lucky's current location.

Lucky wasn't far from Grandma, so she would physically see him, have a vet check him, and if all went well, pay for him and make transportation arrangements. Grandma had already researched horse transportation and knew many options existed. She even knew the cost, which surprisingly wasn't much considering the distance Lucky would travel. Grandma would ask Sadie's parents to pay the transportation costs, so they would have a part to play in welcoming Lucky to the family. Grandma confided in Sadie that if they balked she would pay for transportation, too. Grandma wasn't rich, but according to her, "What could be more important?"

It all went according to plan. Sadie held her breath and anticipated that her parents would be reluctant when hearing of a horse no one had seen yet, especially because he was in California. But, after ensuring that this was what Sadie wanted, they agreed. They even agreed to pay for the transportation! Sadie wasn't sure if her parents agreed so readily because they knew better than to take on Grandma, or if they just simply thought this was the way most people bought horses. She didn't ask. She and Grandma had just sealed the deal on the most beautiful horse Sadie had ever seen...even if she'd only seen him on the computer.

Sadie wasn't sure she'd EVER been this excited and could barely contain herself. If she was just dreaming she didn't want to wake up. This was the closest she'd ever been to owning a horse. She wanted to jump up and down, but reminded herself that Lucky wasn't hers just yet; he still needed a vet check and Grandma needed to meet him in person. But, in her mind, she ran through the beautiful pictures she'd seen of Lucky, one by one. *Please let this be real*, she thought.

****

Grandma arranged to see Lucky the following day, and Sadie halfway wondered if Grandma had already made the arrangements before calling. She told Sadie to contact Mrs. Groen, either by e-mail or phone,

and ask any questions she may have. Grandma confessed
that her horse days were long behind her, but said she
still had an eye for a winner and would be able to tell if
there was anything wrong with Lucky.

Sadie e-mailed Mrs. Groen a list of questions and
introduced herself:

From: Sadie Navarro <wealhm@aol.com>
To: Mrs.Groen <bayequinemom@gmail.com>
Sent: Sun, Aug 8, 2010 1:42 pm
Subject: **Introduction and Questions About Lucky**
Dear Mrs. Groen,

My name is Sadie Navarro, and my grandmother has
been talking to you about your horse, Lucky. She told
me I could go ahead and e-mail you some questions,
and I was hoping you might have time to answer them.
I have a lot, but I'll try to only ask the most important
ones, and the ones for which I don't already have answers:

> Has Lucky been trained enough so that I will be
> able to ride him?
> What discipline of riding is he trained in?
> Is he gentle?

Thank you again for your time.
Sincerely,
Sadie Navarro

Mrs. Groen replied immediately:

From: Mrs. Groen <bayequinemom@gmail.com>
To: Sadie Navarro <wealhm@aol.com>
Sent: Sun, Aug 8, 2010 1:56 pm
Subject: RE: Introduction and Questions About Lucky

Hi Sadie,

Yes, I know who you are. Your grandmother has told me all about you. Here are the answers to your questions:

Lucky has had some training under saddle, and if you ride the way your Grandma says you do, you should be fine. I have trained him in the basic walk, trot, canter, and schooled him over small fences with an English saddle. I have also ridden him in a Western saddle, and he seemed to like it. He's a good boy.

He is very gentle.

You may also want to chat with my daughter, Lauren, who is closer to your age. Lauren's e-mail address is lgroen637@gmail.com, and she is here now. I look forward to meeting your grandmother, and hope she likes Lucky. We do.
> Mrs. Amy Groen

Sadie sent her a note back thanking her, and told her she looked forward to contacting Lauren.

Sadie and Lauren e-mailed a few times and switched to texting. Lauren was very sad Lucky was leaving, but felt better knowing he would be going to a girl who would love him and understand him like she did. Sadie assured her if Lucky came to Maryland that she would take very good care of him, and he would find a special purpose in life. She jokingly texted, to try and make Lauren feel better, "Maybe he'll be a Senator," since they were right near the nation's capital, Washington, D.C.

The next day, Sadie picked up a voicemail on her cell phone when she left the barn, where she'd been making arrangements for her potential horse. Her kindred spirit's voice stated, "Honey, he's even more incredible in person than he was in pictures. We are so lucky to have found him. The vet liked him, too. So I paid Mrs. Groen for him, and he's now yours. Congratulations, sweetie. Oh, and he's grown a little since the ad…maybe more like 16 hands high now. But I'm sure that won't be a problem for you. Give me a call when you get this, love you!"

This time Sadie really did jump up and down! She owned a horse. Her life's dream came true, and she felt a bit stunned. It had all happened so fast.

Her phone rang, bringing her out of her trance.

"I thought I told you to call me!" Grandma said warmly and with a smile in her voice.

"Hi Grandma, I just got your message, and it just, well, took me a minute to process it. Grandma, I own a horse! Can you believe it? How many times have I asked for a pony for my birthday and Christmas? And how many times have I pretended that the horses I rode in lessons at stables were mine? And now it just all seems so unreal. Thank you SO MUCH, Grandma. I'll be forever grateful for all you did," Sadie said.

"I just couldn't wait to tell you everything," Grandma said. "You are going to be so happy, Sadie. He has the kindest eyes and the nicest personality — he's a bundle of love. I can't wait until you see him."

"I can't wait either. Do you know when he'll get here?"

"Well, since I had already talked to a bunch of horse shippers, I lined one up to take him later this week. They said it should take about seven days to move him across the country, with breaks and everything. So, with any luck, you'll be seeing him a week from tomorrow."

Sadie's suspicions regarding Grandma's planning

ahead of time returned. This all seemed to be falling into place very easily. Not that it mattered to Sadie. In fact, she felt elated that her horse would be here so soon. Her horse. She had a horse; his name was Lucky, and he would be arriving in just over a week!

"Thank you again, Grandma. I'll talk to Mom and Dad and let them know. I love you, Grandma, and please catch a wave for me."

"Will do, my girl, and I'll make sure it's a big one. Oh, and one more thing, I took some pictures and e-mailed them to you. Take a look and tell me if you think your Grandma can pick horses. Love you, too, bye now."

Sadie still couldn't believe it. She had her own horse.

ॐ4ॐ

ANTICIPATION

The next seven days seemed to be the longest of Sadie's life. Her anticipation of Lucky's arrival was driving her, and everyone around her, crazy. Austin took Sadie to the bookstore and they bought a book on horse ownership, which she read cover to cover. Sadie was a voracious reader, probably a speed reader when it came to horse books. The book included a checklist of items any new horse owner would need, and she found a horse tack consignment shop not far from their home where she purchased many of the items in used but good condition. She had everything she needed to get started.

Loftmar Stables prepared a stall for Lucky. Outside his stall was a brand new stable card, and Sadie couldn't help but be proud when she read it:

COLOR ME LUCKY
Andalusian/National Show Horse
Tri-color Pinto
OWNER: SADIE NAVARRO

She read the OWNER: SADIE NAVARRO part again and again, letting it sink in and grinning.

The boarders at Loftmar welcomed Sadie and shared their knowledge with her. They advised her to buy a horse blanket only after she actually measured her horse, and to wait to buy a saddle for the same reason. Jessi, her riding instructor and the barn manager, knew how keyed up Sadie was and loaned her a book on horse training, telling her the key was to take it very slowly.

The horse shippers had been in touch with Mr. and Mrs. Navarro during the cross country transit, and assured them Lucky was fine. They couldn't tell the exact date they'd be arriving because they needed to drop off some horses and pick up some others, but everything appeared to be on track.

They finally called with an exact arrival time. Lucky and the trailer would arrive at 8:00 a.m. on Sunday, August 17th.

The Navarros planted themselves outside Loftmar's barn at 7:00 a.m. on Sunday. Sadie checked her lead rope, halter, grooming kit, and anything else she could for the hundredth time.

Dad put his hands on her shoulders, looked her square in the eye, and said, "C'mon, Punkin, you can't wear yourself out before he gets here. It's almost time, and everything is going to be perfect – just like you've been thinking. Tranquiiiilllooo...." he continued, speaking to her in soft and soothing Spanish, something the two of them shared. His words and demeanor calmed her.

Jessi showed up at 7:30 a.m., just a little earlier than normal for the morning feed shift. "Hi, guys," she said brightly, "I like to be here when new horses arrive to help with any issues that might come up."

Five minutes later, they heard a large tractor trailer moving along the gravel road towards the barn and a lone whinny calling to whatever horses would listen.

Sadie knew it was Lucky.

The enormous tractor trailer, which had enough room to haul eighteen horses, pulled up. A man jumped out and introduced himself to Mrs. Navarro as Doug, who she'd been talking to over the past week. *Ugh, quit talking and open the trailer*, thought Sadie. She could hear Lucky crying out inside. So far, no horses had answered him. Doug and Mom finally moved to the rear of the trailer. "Are you ready to take him?" he asked Sadie.

Sadie's heart just about jumped out of her chest. She was too excited to speak, so nodded her head YES! He opened the back trailer doors, and she could see her horse's big, strong hindquarters and a thick black tail that almost reached the trailer floor.

Doug turned Lucky around and, despite his frantic calling, he walked nicely down the ramp. Sadie was in love.

Standing before her was the most magnificent horse she had ever seen, and when she looked into his eyes her heart skipped a beat at how kind, expressive, and intelligent they were.

She was a little taken aback by his size, but it did not scare her. She took the lead rope from Doug and calmly led Lucky through the barn doors and into his stall. His ears darted around as he took in his new surroundings, but he walked nicely beside her. When they got to the stall, Sadie removed the halter and handed it back to Doug.

While Sadie's Mom and Doug exchanged paper-work, made final payments, and talked about the best way to back the trailer out of the driveway, Sadie stood in complete awe of her new best friend. A few of the barn horses gave welcoming whinnies to Lucky, and he whinnied back, seemingly glad to be with other horses again. Sadie knew that most horses didn't like to be alone because they are herd animals, and understood why Lucky had been unhappy for the last leg of his trip. He seemed to be settling in, which was amazing since it had only been a few minutes.

It surprised Sadie when she turned around and found Miss Jan, the barn owner, standing outside Lucky's stall. Miss Jan and her husband had owned Loftmar Stables since 1984 and lived on the property. They noticed the giant trailer pulling in, and Miss Jan came to see the new horse. She admittedly was not a fan of boarding young horses because they tend to get into trouble, but for some reason, she had said "yes" to Sadie. Maybe because they were neighbors.

Miss Jan said, "So let's see what we have here. Let's turn him out in the indoor arena and let him stretch a little bit. He's been cooped up in that trailer for days and needs to move."

Sadie was a bit nervous about this. She didn't think Lucky had ever even seen an indoor arena, and now he was going into one for the first time with the barn owner handling him. This might not be pretty. But, there was only one way to find out, and something Sadie had learned in her short time at Loftmar was that when Miss Jan spoke, people listened. Sadie walked into Lucky's stall, patted him on his neck, and slipped his new halter on. She started to lead him out of his stall, and Miss Jan said, "I've got him."

It always amazed Sadie to watch extremely experienced horse people. Horses know right away that these people know what to do. Miss Jan led Lucky into the indoor arena, let him stop and look around for a minute, and then detached his lead rope to let him wander around. The first thing he did was follow her, and she laughed. She said, "Go ahead and be a horse, you, and get some exercise." Then she left the arena. Miss Jan and Sadie watched Lucky from the gate, and he stood there looking at them, letting out a small whinny. He turned, trotted away, and started exploring things in the arena that he had likely never seen before, such as jumps, fake trees, and highway cones.

Please don't eat the flowers and trees, Sadie thought, still not knowing what this young horse might do. Lucky walked around a bit, trotted some more, stretched his neck out, and seemed to fit right in. Miss Jan watched and smiled, and Sadie thought that Miss Jan just might like this young horse after all.

"Let's take him outside and let him meet another horse so he can play," Miss Jan said.

So far, so good, and Sadie felt so fortunate to have both Miss Jan and Jessi there on Lucky's first day.

Blue, one of the younger horses at the barn, was already out in the geldings' field when Miss Jan released Lucky. The two found each other immediately and started a horse-meeting routine, which included snorting, stomping and squealing. That was all it took for them to sort out their herd dynamics, and after a few minutes, the two horses romped in the field as if they had been buddies forever. They ran, played halter tag, stopped, snorted, stomped and squealed again. Blue rolled in the dirt, so Lucky rolled in the dirt, and then they both stood up and shook off. Miss Jan looked at Sadie and said, "I think he's going to be fine. I think you've got a nice horse there."

Sadie was floored. A compliment from Miss Jan, who had been in the horse business her entire life, meant a lot. Miss Jan didn't give gratuitous compliments. She meant what she said. Even though Sadie had wanted to spend the first few hours alone with her horse, grooming and babying him, and telling him how wonderful he was, she was grateful for the experienced wisdom of Jessi and Miss Jan. She knew that Lucky should be doing exactly what he was doing right now, not standing in a stall.

Mom, Dad, and Austin eventually wandered home, while Sadie savored every minute she could watching her new horse. She knew she was biased, but she thought he had the most spectacular movements she'd ever seen. His flexibility amazed her, and he turned on a dime. As she watched, it was almost as if she could tell what he was thinking. "*Hey, Blue, watch this,*" and he'd run to the far end of the field at full speed and then come to a screeching halt, turning back to look at Blue. He was so animated, and she knew it would be a great pleasure to watch him for hours on end.

Sadie's mom called her cell phone a few hours later and told her she had to come home. That was reasonable, and Lucky didn't seem to need her. She had hoped to be able to brush him, but she knew she could brush him tomorrow. After all, he was her horse and she could see him every day. Right now he needed to settle, and he was enjoying his new friend Blue. Over the course of several hours, Jessi had let a few more horses out into the geldings' field, one at a time, to help acquaint them with their new herd mate. So far, all was fine, and even if Sadie stayed there, she wouldn't change the herd dynamics. So, although she would have rather stayed all day and all night, she followed her mom's directions and went home.

Mom made a special dinner that night in honor of Lucky's arrival: Dad's favorite meal, chicken enchiladas, with traditional beans and rice, and even a carrot cake for dessert in honor of Lucky. Sadie saved a piece to give to him. During dinner they talked about how blessed they were to have Lucky and how well everything was turning out.

****

Towards the end of dinner, Dad said he had some news. His deployment date to Afghanistan would be the following Sunday. Before this announcement, this had been the best day of Sadie's life. Stunned, she realized now that somehow she was going to have to cope with Dad's absence and the gnawing worry over his safety. He would be in an extremely dangerous place for at least a year. Lucky didn't know it, but he already had a purpose in life - to help Sadie through it all.

༄5༄

GETTING TO KNOW YOU

Sadie walked back to the barn first thing Monday morning and found Lucky munching hay in his stall. She greeted him enthusiastically, and he looked at her with a sense of curious recognition. Sadie grabbed her brush box with all her new grooming tools and got ready to give him the brushing of a lifetime.

She picked up the curry comb, a rough comb used to loosen dirt and bring it to the top of the horse's coat so it could be brushed off later. But when she entered his stall and approached him, he backed away from her. She remembered Jessi's advice to take things slow, backed up, and approached him again, this time much slower. She also let him sniff the curry comb, and her, to let him get used to her being there with something in her hand.

She started with very slow, circular strokes on the left side, or "near" side, of Lucky's neck. Lucky reacted to the curry comb and pulled away again. This was not going as planned.

Sadie retreated to her grooming box and decided she would not follow the traditional routine of starting with a curry comb, then a hard brush, and then a soft brush. Instead she went straight for the soft brush. Moving slowly, and talking in a soft low voice, she let Lucky sniff the brush as she started to groom him with it. He looked at her with what she took as an approval of the soft brush.

Sadie smoothed all the hairs in Lucky's coat with what seemed like one thousand strokes. He kept his eye on her, looking up from his hay as she moved. He let out a snort or two, but overall seemed to accept his beauty treatment. When Sadie finished one side, she decided to move around in front of him rather than behind. Lucky was a nice horse, but Sadie didn't know if he might kick out because of the newness of having her in his space. Not to mention, there were flies in the barn and Sadie didn't want to accidentally get kicked if Lucky thought she was a fly back there.

As she started on his right, or "off", side she realized again just how big he was. She had never groomed or ridden a horse this big!

"You know, Lucky," she said to him, "I have never groomed or ridden a horse as big as you. I know you are really nice, but I ask you to be gentle with me, please." Lucky just ate his hay.

Sadie was tall for her age and was able to brush the top of his back when she stood on her tip toes. He looked back at her, and she thought she saw him grin. She continued around his side, careful to brush his legs ever so gently since he appeared to be a little ticklish.

Even though she hadn't gone through the normal brushing routine, Sadie decided her improvisation was good, so her new horse could get used to her. Even with her condensed routine, he still shone like silver in the sun. Lucky had a nice soft summer coat. It needed some currying to remove the dust he had rolled in yesterday with Blue, but Sadie was convinced that small steps were okay for now. He still needed to get to know her.

Picking out horses' hooves is one of the most important aspects of horse care. Too many kids at the barn didn't pick their horses' feet because it could be hard to do, but it is extremely important for the horses' hoof care and for safety. Little rocks and dirt can get lodged in the horses' hooves, and if unattended, can make them very sore or lame. Sadie assumed Lucky was used to having his feet picked out since he had come from a good home, but she did understand it might be a challenge since he didn't really know or trust her yet.

She retrieved the hoof pick from her grooming box and let Lucky sniff it, as she had the other tools. He seemed disinterested, so she moved to his near side and picked up his left front hoof, facing his tail like she had been taught, she picked the mud and dirt out of his hoof.

"Good boy," she said.

He had nice hard feet.

"I'm going to talk to Matt, the farrier, about your feet, Lucky, next time he comes to the barn," she said.

She regularly watched Matt and admired him for his patience with her twenty questions, and with the horses. Matt always quoted a famous saying, "No hoof, no horse."

Sadie moved to the back left hoof, and Lucky picked up and held his hoof just like he was supposed to.

This was going better than she had planned. A quick pick, and without thinking she moved behind him to pick the other back hoof.

As she picked up his right hind hoof, he kicked out, which caught Sadie completely off guard! She landed on her left side and banged her head on the stall wall. The next thing she knew, Lucky's nose was in her face and he seemed to be wondering, "What are you doing down there?"

Sadie got up and dusted off, feeling a little unsure of herself.

"I guess it was a fly," Sadie reasoned to herself. A little dizzy, she stood there for a minute and patted Lucky's neck. She decided to leave the back right hoof alone and move to the right front one. She carefully moved her hand down Lucky's front leg to let him know she was there and to ask him to pick up his hoof, which he did. As she was picking, he snorted and left a small trail of gunk on her behind! She jumped a little, still a bit shaky from the last hoof.

"Great. First he kicks me, then he sneezes on me," she said.

Then she realized that Lucky was gently nudging her, perhaps saying he was sorry for having kicked out. But maybe not for sneezing!

Sadie was a problem solver, so she immediately had to figure out why Lucky had kicked. It could have been a fly, but perhaps that was a convenient explanation. She thought about it and realized that Lucky couldn't see she was behind him because horses have a blind spot directly behind them, right where she had been. While she had followed all hoof picking protocols on Lucky's first two legs - gently touching his legs and leaning slightly into him so he would shift his weight off the hoof about to be picked - she skipped those steps on the right hind hoof. She admitted to herself that she was a little distracted when she moved behind him and didn't think to talk to him or to touch his leg. She had just grabbed the hoof. Lesson learned. It wasn't Lucky's fault; he was just being a horse and defending himself from what he instinctively thought might be a danger.

Okay, so far so good. Lucky had already been a teacher to Sadie, and Sadie had taught Lucky that she was a safe person, even when carrying grooming tools. The human-horse interaction had been a success.

****

Jessi didn't normally teach lessons on Monday mornings, but she happened to be at the barn feeding horses. Sadie pleaded with her, "Jessi, can you PLEASE give me a lesson today?"

"Okay, I want to see how this new horse goes anyway. Meet me in the arena in one hour."

Sadie figured it would take the full hour to slowly introduce Lucky to his new tack, but she took a short break, called her mom, and let her know how well it was going with Lucky. Of course, she conveniently left out the part about the kick.

Just as Sadie predicted, tacking up for the first time took every bit of the time she allotted. Lucky had been ridden in an English saddle and bridle, but he questioned every piece of equipment she pulled out and gave it a thorough inspection with his eyes and nose. He was tolerant, but also quite wary.

"Okay," she said. "We have an hour before our

lesson. We'll take our time."

Sadie was careful to introduce each piece of equipment only after Lucky was relaxed. She also took extra time to adjust everything to fit him, since it was his first time wearing his new tack. Sadie had studied all the bridle and saddle fitting measurements from her new book, and had even brought the book with her in case she needed to look something up. Thankfully, Jessi would double check all her work. Exactly one hour after she started, she led him out of his stall for their lesson.

Jessi was waiting in the indoor arena, and Sadie was thankful once again that Miss Jan had been there yesterday and introduced Lucky to the arena. At least he was a little familiar with the place where they would have their first ride. Jessi checked all the tack, made a few minor adjustments, and asked Sadie to walk Lucky around the arena to help get him relaxed.

"We were in here yesterday," Sadie mentioned, anxious to just get on and ride.

"I know you were, but it's important that Lucky learn to trust and respect you, and that's something that happens through groundwork, working with the horse from the ground."

Sadie obliged Jessi. *I'll be very disappointed if I don't get to ride Lucky in today's lesson,* she thought.

Jessi gave Sadie commands to walk, turn, and halt Lucky in both directions. Lucky was dragging Sadie around the arena and not listening at all well. Jessi demonstrated to Sadie several ways of handling him that would improve her control from the ground, and Sadie watched Lucky behave much better when Jessi used the techniques. Sadie tried to follow Jessi's example, but Lucky was still leading Sadie instead of the other way around. A few helpful corrections from Jessi, and Lucky began to listen just a little. The fact was that Sadie was new at this, and Lucky could sense her uncertainty. On top of that, Sadie could feel herself getting upset; there was a much bigger reason she wanted to ride than just getting on her new horse.

"I told you this would not be a quick process," Jessi said, in her instructor voice. "That book I loaned you will help you a lot with the theory and step-by-step instruction of groundwork. I know you just want to get on and ride, but the horse must respect you on the ground. Or it's not going to go well."

Sadie couldn't help it; she burst into tears and the bigger reason came out. "But I've got to show my dad I can ride Lucky before he leaves for Afghanistan on Sunday!"

Jessi softened. "Oh, Sadie! Is that because your dad actually told you that, or because you told yourself that?" Jessi asked.

Choking back her sniffles, Sadie whimpered, "No, he didn't say that. It's just that I got the horse because we moved here, and he's going so soon, and if he doesn't see me ride him before he goes….well," and another burst of tears, "…he may never see me ride him."

"All right, Sadie, let's calm down. Remember, horses can tell when you are upset, and right now Lucky knows you are upset. Take a few deep breaths, and let's walk Lucky around a little more. I have an idea that I think will work."

They spent the next five minutes walking Lucky, letting him look around, and talking about things. Even though Jessi said Lucky knew Sadie was upset, Sadie couldn't see it. All she knew was that he was being a brat when she tried to lead him, and because of that, Jessi wasn't going to let her ride him in her lesson. First the kick, and now this. *Where is Grandma Collins now?*

"We're going to take this nice and easy, okay? Now I know it's been a long time since anyone has used a lead rope with you while you ride, but that's how we're going to start with Lucky. So wait right here, and I'll come back with a halter and lead line. That way, I can have some control, and you will be safe. I can also teach him some respect from the ground while you are mounted. He may be perfectly fine, but I want to make sure." Jessi left to fetch the equipment.

Sadie walked Lucky to the wall-mounted mounting block in the arena, and he backed up right away, startled. As Jessi returned, she said, "Come on over here. Lots of the new horses are afraid of that mounting block because they've never seen one like it. Let's use the mobile one until he gets used to it."

Once again Sadie was feeling like she was in over her head with this horse training; she had no idea it would be this hard. What did the Native Americans do in the old days? They didn't have choices of mounting blocks, or lead lines...or maybe they did, but they just called them something different. Anyhow, back to the task at hand, Sadie walked Lucky up to the mobile mounting block, and he stood still. When she moved to his side, and stepped onto the mounting block, he moved his hindquarters as far as he could away from her. Now she was feeling like a complete failure.

"Don't worry about that. You really haven't taught him what you want yet, so you can't punish him for not doing it. I want you to walk him up to it again, tell him "Whoa," and stroke him on the side of his neck a few times," Jessi instructed.

Sadie followed Jessi's directions, and this time he stood politely.

Jessi continued, "Now, very nonchalantly, I want you to step on the first step of the mounting block, and stop. We're doing this one step at a time. There, that's it. Now stroke his neck again, and talk to him nice and easy."

And step by step with a little give and take and many more trips to the mounting block, Sadie finally had him standing still through the whole process, including putting his reins over his head.

"Now Sadie, I could have just held him for you after the first time, and you would have been able to get on. But I'm showing you what I mean when I talk about trust and respect. All I would have taught him was to stand when I held him. He needs to know to stand nicely when YOU want him to stand. And you've come one step closer to that today. Now I'll warn you, he's young, and he may forget all about this lesson tomorrow. So don't get discouraged, just be firm and consistent." Sadie was so thankful to have such an experienced riding instructor.

Getting on Lucky went smoothly; he didn't move. Jessi instructed Sadie to gently squeeze with her legs to ask him to go forward. She reminded her that it was best to start with subtle commands, and to use bigger aids like a kick only if her horse did not respond to lighter aids. Lucky moved off her leg easily and had a nice forward walk. He was not pulling on the reins, and he followed Jessi while she walked at his shoulder. They executed a halt, and this was clearly a command he understood. She encouraged him to walk forward again, and he did so with another gentle squeeze. Maybe this wasn't going to be so bad after all.

They only had a few minutes left, and Jessi asked if Sadie wanted to trot. Sadie thought, *well, I'd really like to canter him,* but trusting her instructor, she nodded and said, "Yes." A little squeeze and a cluck, and Lucky eased into a slow smooth trot. Jessi jogged along side with her eyes on both Sadie and Lucky. Sadie wasn't crying now. She was grinning from ear to ear. Jessi said, "Don't look down, look ahead, and don't forget your posting diagonals," meaning rising when Lucky's outside front leg went forward and sitting when his inside front leg went forward.

Jessi asked her to slow to a walk, and then a halt. They stood in the middle of the arena and talked for a minute, and Sadie dismounted. It was a long way down. "Thank you, Jessi, for all the training," Sadie beamed. She had much more confidence that she would be able to ride for her dad before he left.

As she began walking Lucky back to his stall, she peeked outside and saw one of the other boarders, Jimmy, in the outdoor arena. She decided to take Lucky out there and say, "Hello." Jimmy was a few years older than Sadie and had a Quarter Horse named Billy, who was a racing Quarter Horse turned hunter/jumper. She didn't know Jimmy well, but he was always friendly. And, kind of cute.

"Why are you standing out there? Come on in," he invited.

Sadie unlatched the gate and walked Lucky over to where Billy was standing. Billy and Lucky sniffed each other and pawed the ground, and Sadie backed Lucky away.

"Hey, I'd like to see you ride him – a new horse and all," Jimmy said.

Even though something gnawed at her inside and told her not to, Sadie said, "Sure." So she walked Lucky over to the mounting block, steadied him, and hopped on. *Well*, she thought, *today's training went well. This will be a piece of cake.*

She urged Lucky forward as he looked around at his new surroundings; he'd never been in the outdoor arena. Just then a big bird swooped right down in front of Lucky's face, and he spun around in a 360 degree turn to get away from it, losing his rider.

Sadie felt herself hit the ground, and the next thing she knew, she woke up to Jessi's face. "How many fingers am I holding up?"

Sadie answered, "Two," the correct number, and Jessi helped her up from the ground.

"What happened?" Sadie asked, still dazed.

"What happened is that you thought you could do more than you should have. Geez, Sadie, I didn't think I had to tell you not to ride Lucky on your own yet. You need a little more supervised time with me. Don't be in such a rush. I'll be with you when you ride him for your dad before he leaves for Afghanistan, and please don't try to do this again until I tell you it's safe. Thank goodness you didn't get hurt," Jessi said. Sadie could see that she was not happy with her – at all.

Jimmy was in the background holding Billy and Lucky. "I'm sorry; I really didn't know that there had been issues with him already. I wouldn't have asked you to ride him. I've had my fair share of thrills and spills with Billy, so don't feel alone. It'll be okay. We'll ride again someday when you get him under control," he said apologetically.

Under control!? As she remembered it, a giant bird, a blue heron she thought, swooped down in front of her. It wasn't a control issue. *Well, maybe it was. Maybe I shouldn't have taken him into the outdoor arena where there are so many unfamiliar obstacles.* Sadie couldn't wait to put Lucky away, go home, and try to figure out why everything she was doing with him was so wrong.

When she got home, Sadie dialed Grandma Collins and told her about the day, letting the tears out when she felt like it. Grandma sympathized and told her she needed to look for the signs that would help her and Lucky be in harmony. She said the Irish always believed in signs, and they could come in various shapes and sizes, but they were always there. Grandma was convinced that once Sadie found the signs, all would be well. *Great.*

Sadie texted Lauren: "Lauren, did you have any issues with Lucky kicking out, disrespecting you, or spooking at things? SN"

"SN – No," came the reply text. "Never had any problems, but maybe he's just afraid with everything being so new. Good luck, Lauren."

Great. Again, Sadie was left to deduce from her day that she was a terrible rider, a bad horse trainer, a show off, in way over her head, and had no good solution for her problems. All she had were her grandmother's words, "Look for the signs."

Her fleeting joy had turned to heartbreak.

๛6๛

THE SIGNS

Sadie thought all night and tried and tried to find her grandmother's "signs."

The next morning, she stared into Lucky's eyes waiting for some kind of epiphany. She listened to his whinnies thinking maybe there was something in his voice. She checked his hooves to see if there was some hidden clue. And although she felt very foolish, she checked every square inch of his stall to see if there was something there, thinking back to a book she had once read about a spider who weaved a special message into the corner of a pig's stall. Although there were spiders, there were certainly no special signs.

Austin knew Sadie was perplexed. At first, Sadie didn't think it would be much help to tell him how distraught she was over this silliness with the "signs." But she finally decided to give him a shot since she didn't have many other places to turn. He knew Grandma as well as she did, so he clearly understood her Irish beliefs and convictions. Austin's response: "I'll help."

With newfound hope, Sadie dragged Austin to the barn. Although he had been to barns many times before, he had never had an important "horse" purpose. He usually put up with the horses, and the people, just waiting until his little sister said it was time to go. Today was different.

Austin surveyed Lucky as if it was the first time he'd seen him. Lucky leaned over and nuzzled Austin affectionately and let out a small whinny. Austin always had a way with animals; they somehow sensed he was their friend. As Austin petted Lucky, he viewed every square inch of his 250 square foot body. He stroked his hair and ran his fingers through his mane and tail, lightly combing them. Lucky whinnied again in what sounded like a small laugh in reaction to a tickle. All this was well and good, but Sadie wasn't seeing any "signs."

It began at his face. Austin, standing eye to eye with Lucky. A six foot tall boy and a 16 hand high horse.

"It starts here," he said.

Austin ran his hand gently from the top of the white blaze on Lucky's forehead down to his warm breathing nostrils. "I," he said.

He moved his hand along the left side of Lucky's face and followed his brown pinto markings along the curves into what appeared to be a "B." He turned to Sadie and smiled — a perfect Austin smile conveying that nothing made him happier than to make other people happy. Sadie smiled back, pushing it a little, since she wasn't sure what she was supposed to be so happy about or what Austin was on to. Something she had learned, though, from spending her entire life as Austin's sister, was to be patient. And so she patiently waited for this mystery to unfold.

Austin continued his slow, deliberate stroking of Lucky's coat and next announced "E," as he traced the letter E on Lucky's markings. Sadie watched, totally enthralled at what her brother was finding in this beautiful pinto's markings. She had stared and stared at this horse for hours on end and had never seen such things. He continued down the horse's left shoulder and pointed out what to him seemed to be an obvious "L." Sadie wanted to kick herself for not having seen this. But then again, she was happy to see her brother getting such delight from helping her.

And so it went. Austin's declarations became stronger with each letter. "I," he exclaimed. He drew out the next "E," then "V," and then a final "E." He turned to Sadie and said, "That's it."

Sadie's heart raced as she put it all together. She wasn't sure what she felt - curiosity, astonishment, or disbelief. She now had a clear sign. A sign beyond what she could ever have imagined. "I Believe" marked on her horse.

Sadie and Austin had spent hours over the years lying on their backs finding pictures in the clouds. Austin was always much better than Sadie at finding hidden trees, animals, and shapes. Today Austin's ability to see meaning in natural patterns had changed her life, she was quite sure. Overwhelmed with emotion, Sadie threw her arms around Austin, squeezed him and burst into happy tears.

"Thank you, my best brother in the world. I don't even know what this means yet, but I know I could never have done this without you. Everyone should be so lucky to have a brother like you," Sadie managed to speak through the tears.

Austin hugged her back, shrugged, and turned to stroke Lucky, again retracing the "sign" that he had so cleverly discovered. Then, he turned to Sadie and said, "Time for me to go now?" That brother of hers, he certainly was one of a kind! Sadie laughed and said "Good bye" to Austin. She herself was staying at the barn.

Not quite sure what to do with her newfound sign, she wanted to stay with Lucky and ponder it. So, when Austin left, she turned, looked Lucky in the eye and said out loud, "I believe." She felt ridiculous, but somehow, it was the right thing to do.

Once again, tears came to her eyes as she felt something very profound had just happened.

⁓7⁓

ENCOUNTERING A MISSION

Throughout the week, Jessi helped Sadie learn horsemanship with her new four-legged companion. None of the days were as eventful as the first, and Sadie felt as if she and Lucky were beginning to understand each other. She followed Jessi's advice and carefully studied the principles in the book Jessi loaned her. Patience, consistency, trust, and respect drove Sadie's actions on the ground and in the saddle. She was building a strong relationship with her horse. Sadie whispered "I believe" to Lucky first thing each time she visited and whenever she got flustered. That wasn't in the book, but it seemed to be working for her.

Jessi dispensed with the lead line after Wednesday's session, and following two successful lessons on Thursday and Friday, Jessi felt Sadie was secure enough to ride Lucky on her own for her dad on Saturday. Sadie wanted this ride to be special for her dad, so she asked if dad could come on his own. Her mom understood, aware of their special father-daughter bond and the upcoming departure. Besides, she'd be there to watch for many other rides.

Sadie adored her dad, even if horses weren't his thing. They both loved reading, learning, and could talk for hours about how they thought the world should be. Dad had a tremendous vocabulary, and taught Sadie new words both in English and in Spanish. He also had what she considered a photographic memory, as he seemed to remember every famous quote he ever heard, who said it, and why it was important. She thought he had to be the smartest man in the world.

But it wasn't all about learning. She and Dad had other special customs that had become "theirs" over the years. With every move, they went on a quest for the best Chinese restaurant in town. For them, the more obscure, the better. Mom and Austin weren't interested in this search and didn't even like Chinese food, which Sadie didn't understand. So far, with every move, they had found the perfect Chinese cuisine after a series of taste tests at local establishments. They'd only tried one here in Bowie so far, and they both agreed that the quest was not over. Sadie tried not to think about how long it would be before they could find "their" next taste of China here in Maryland.

Chinese food was the last thing on her mind on Saturday morning. A tad nervous, she tacked Lucky up, talking to him as she did.

"Lucky," she explained, "this is a really important ride. Dad is leaving for.... well, for awhile after this, and I really want him to see what we can do. Please,

please be good today."

Sadie entered the arena with Dad watching from the gate. Jessi gave her a knowing look and winked, putting Sadie more at ease. As if in a show, Sadie confidently walked Lucky to the wall mounting block and got on without a hitch. She sensed Lucky understood something was different about this ride. Jessi stood in the center and called off commands which Sadie and Lucky executed as if they had been a team for years. They walked, trotted, and cantered in both directions, performed turns on the forehand and haunches, halted square, and even trotted a few small cross rail jumps. Sadie then directed Lucky to where her dad was standing, and asked, "What do you think?"

"I think I can't wait to see what you will be doing in a year," Dad said proudly. Although she knew he knew nothing of the maneuvers she had performed, he was choking back tears at the sight of his daughter on her horse. She and Dad were the emotional ones in the family, and they knew it.

To keep the waterworks from flowing, Sadie trotted off and said, "Let me show you how he jumps again, so you don't forget. We've only done it a few times, and he's going to get so much better. I'll send you some videos of our progress after you leave." She caught a lump in her throat as she said those last words, but quickly continued. "I need to get better, too," she said, trying to inject some humor. Sadie jumped a few small jumps, patted Lucky, and walked him around to ensure he cooled down. She and Dad continued chatting and smiling back and forth. Back at the stall, Dad watched while she brushed Lucky down, and then she let Lucky out to go play with his horse friends. "Thank you

Lucky," she said as she let him go.

All had gone well.

****

Sunday came. The time to say "Goodbye."

Mom tried to stay strong, but Sadie could see the strain in her face. She heard Mom speaking to Dad, thinking the kids couldn't hear her.

"I know we've been through Navy deployments, and I know about separation. But this time it's different. You'll be gone longer, and it's more dangerous, and...." Her words trailed off as Mom seemed to be searching for an answer.

Dad tried to console her and buried her head in his shoulder saying, "Sssshhhh, now, everything is going to be just fine, don't worry about me."

Austin didn't say much, but Sadie knew he took it hard.

Dad turned to Austin. "Austin, remember, you need to be the man of the house while I'm gone." Then, he winked and said, "But don't get too used to it, because I'll be taking the job back when I return," trying to show some levity.

"And you, young lady," he said, turning to Sadie, "keep up the great work with Lucky. Who knows, maybe even your Mexican cowboy Dad might hop up on him when I get back?" This surprised Sadie, because even though she knew Dad loved animals, he'd never expressed an interest in riding.

The family packed into the car and took Dad to the base where he would meet up with his unit and fly to Afghanistan.

Before she knew it, the family hugged and kissed goodbye and all went their ways, trying to stay brave.

Sadie couldn't help but look back one more time as they left, and saw Dad give her the "thumbs up" sign that had been his signature "All is well" for as long as she could remember. She returned the sign and tried to look cheerful, although she knew he saw through it.

It was a quiet drive home. As soon as they arrived, Austin asked if he could borrow the car to go for a ride, and Sadie asked to go to the barn.

Mom agreed, "Yes, go ahead, but bring your phones in case I need to track you down."

Sadie felt bad leaving her mom by herself, but she also sensed that she needed to be alone so she didn't have to continue to be brave in front of them. Sadie didn't know where Austin was headed, but he was comfortable working things out on his own, so she suspected he was going somewhere to exercise or people watch. All she knew was that she needed to be with Lucky.

She was happy to see other people at the barn. Jimmy and another boarder, Casey, were getting ready to go on a trail ride.

Jimmy asked, "Hey, do you think Lucky can go on the trail?"

Sadie quickly answered, "I think so, as long as you don't take off galloping."

"We never gallop on the trail, and since it will be Lucky's first time out, we'll take it real easy," Jimmy answered.

Although they didn't say anything, Sadie figured Jimmy and Casey knew her dad had left for Afghanistan today. Word travelled quickly at the barn.

Admittedly anxious, Sadie tacked up Lucky and

had a pep talk with him about the trail. It wouldn't be any different than the arena, except there would be trees and an occasional animal or two. And it would be out in the open. Then she remembered the swooping bird, and it unnerved her. Lucky seemed to understand that this was a hard day for Sadie, and he gave her a gentle nudge.

"I believe, I believe, I believe," she repeated, and led him, tacked up, to where Jimmy and Casey were waiting. They asked her if she had been talking to somebody, and Sadie answered, "Of course, to Lucky," and smiled.

The three set out on the trail riding single file, with Sadie in the back of the line. Sadie felt the summer heat and thought about how different the weather was here than in California. She almost never broke a sweat on a ride in San Diego, and here they were barely five minutes out and she was glistening. Casey's voice interrupted her thoughts.

"I'm sorry about your dad having to go away, Sadie," she said, while turning around to speak to her.

Jimmy's head turned on a swivel, and Sadie saw the look he gave Casey. If the look had words, it would have said, "Nice going! We're supposed to be making her forget about that." Of course, Casey was still looking at Sadie, not Jimmy, so the look had no effect on Casey.

Sadie pretended not to see Jimmy's look, which clearly wasn't meant for her, and responded, "Thank you, Casey. I'm sorry, too, but it's nice to know that people care."

Jimmy thought he'd save the day by announcing, "Deer flies! Hope everyone thought to use bug spray. They're awful this time of year. Hopefully we'll get through this patch soon."

Although Jimmy's way of dealing with her dad's

departure was different than Casey's, it still warmed Sadie's heart that each of them cared about her feelings at this difficult time in her life.

The trail ride turned out much less scary than Sadie thought it would be, and Lucky proved a champ. He'd obviously done this in his limited riding time in California because he took everything in stride. He hesitated a bit at a small stream, but readily followed Billy and RJ, Casey's horse, across. Lucky's ears moved to and fro showing he was paying attention to his surroundings, but Sadie could feel that his body was relaxed. If he was nervous, it wasn't obvious. Sadie loved trail riding! To have a successful and fun first trail ride on Lucky was an absolute gift to her.

They returned to the barn, with Sadie elated over Lucky's performance. She also enjoyed getting to know her two barn mates better and appreciated their reaching out to her by inviting her on their trail ride. After the boarders left for the day, Sadie remained, just wanting to bond more with Lucky in the quiet of the empty barn. She brushed him and brushed him, using all the brushes this time, painted his hooves with hoof oil, completely detangled his mane and tail, and hugged him as hard as she could. Grandma had been right; he was the perfect horse.

Sadie pulled out her cell phone and started telling Lucky the story of how she got him, and how glad she was that she hadn't settled for any other horse. She showed Lucky his pictures, ones she had saved on her phone, including the one from his classified ad. Always curious and into everything, he poked around her phone with his nose, and seemed surprised when he made it beep. He backed off, and Sadie laughed. Then he poked the phone again!

"BEEEEEEP."

Sadie thought, *how funny, a horse of my generation who wants to use the cell phone.*

Sadie's phone had internet capability, so she began to show him some of the other classified ads she'd seen, and how many horses were out there.

"I'm warning you, Lucky, try not to be disturbed by what you are about to see. There are some things on the internet about horse auctions that are not pretty."

Sadie had come across web sites during her research that discussed the fate of many auction horses, and she couldn't believe what she read. People were selling horses for human consumption overseas; horsemeat was considered a delicacy in some places. She was amazed and sickened by how many horses are stolen in the United States alone each year, and potentially slaughtered for foreign markets. Many horses are bought at auction and sent to other countries for slaughter. Often, those horses spend their last days being transported in trailers not meant for horses, with no food or water. Even for horses that were lucky enough to escape becoming someone's meal, many of their destinations often lacked good care, and the horses certainly weren't treated as companions.

Sadie started to feel a bit light headed. She figured it must be the August heat, and reminded herself she should take water on her next trail ride when it was this hot.

Lucky watched attentively and startled a bit when a video with sound began to play of one of the auctions. She and Lucky watched the horses at the auction, and then the screen switched to a group of horses in what appeared to be an auction holding pen.

They were there clear as day. Ten horses and ponies of almost every shape and color, and they all seemed to know their fate. Hardball, the Tennessee Walking Horse; Chance, the Arabian; Goliath, the Draft horse; Thor, the Draft cross breed; Lucy and Ricky, the two grade ponies; Buster and Vixen, the two Thoroughbreds; Sunny, the Quarter Horse; and Spot, the Appaloosa. How did she know so much about them? But she did. Was there an audio explaining it? She couldn't tell. All Sadie knew was that she was transfixed by this scene, and Lucky couldn't take his eyes off it either.

Each of the horses had a history, and Sadie wanted to find a rewind button so she could hear the particulars again. But she had no control over the video.

All the horses now were facing the same direction and looking straight at her. Ten pairs of eyes in various stages of fear, desperation, and sadness, all watching Sadie, seemingly pleading for her to do something. Not knowing what else to do, she spoke into the phone.

"Don't worry, everyone, Lucky and I will save you. I don't know how we'll do it, but I believe we can find a way. We promise."

And Lucky whinnied again, as if to second her emotion.

With that, the horses and ponies turned away from the screen. Sadie even thought she saw two of them begin to play.

Sadie realized again just how faint she was feeling, and realized she might be dehydrated, too. She blinked, and decided to sit down for a minute. She rested her head against the side of Lucky's stall and dozed off. Lucky's soft muzzle woke her up. He was sniffing her, as if to ask if she was okay. When she spoke, he stepped back.

"Lucky, did this really just happen?"

Lucky pawed the ground, snorted and shook his head – all perfectly normal horse behaviors. Then he nudged her hand, which still clasped the cell phone. Curious horse behavior. Sadie opened her hand and looked at the screen, and it was a freeze frame of the last scene she remembered. She followed the internet trail to a horse trader, and she had to call.

Sounding a bit foggy, Sadie asked, "Is this really a place that holds horses for auctions?"

"Yes, and don't call back. If you want horses, show up at Hamilton Auction November 11th," a gruff voice on the other end of the line grumbled.

Lucky's ears pricked forward, as he looked at Sadie.

"Don't worry, Lucky, we'll take care of the horses," Sadie assured him.

She finally stood up and steadied herself. She really was not yet used to heat and humidity, and it had been a rather emotional few weeks. She took Lucky out to play with the other horses in the pasture. She drank a bottle of water and thought again about what just happened. She needed to tell her mom, but she didn't want to burden her dad just yet.

Sadie walked home slowly, gathering her thoughts and wondering how to present her experience in a believable way. She was a young girl, determined to somehow rescue ten horses. She had already called the auction site, but she needed her mom's confidence, support, and help to keep the promise she had so sincerely made.

Sadie found her mom outside gardening. No surprise, because her mother found gardening peaceful and meaningful, and it allowed her to think. Sadie thought, *Gardens can be magical. There's no better place to tell Mom about the "encounter" than here.* Sadie's mom looked up as she heard, "Hi Mom, got a minute?"

Sadie told the story as thoroughly as she could, explaining it with as much detail as possible. She described the experience as an "encounter." Her mom weeded an entire section and moved to another before Sadie finished. As she listened, she thought to herself how much Sadie was like her grandmother, the Irish storyteller.

In the end she said, "That's quite a story, Sadie, and I'm wondering if there is something you want to do."

Sadie answered triumphantly, "Take on the mission. We have to save those horses; Lucky and I promised!"

Sadie's mom looked at her daughter standing there before her. A young girl who had just left a life and people she loved, and who only hours earlier had said "Goodbye" to her dad for perhaps the last time. She could easily have dismissed her and this wild tale of rescuing ten horses. Ten horses! But she couldn't break her daughter's heart. Not now. Not today. So instead she said, "All right, Sadie, we'll look into it. And I agree that we shouldn't talk to Dad about this right now. He has enough on his mind. But I'll bet Grandma Collins would love to hear the story."

Early the next morning, Sadie's mom, unbeknownst to Sadie, phoned their new family physician, Dr. Paul, who had already seen Sadie once this week after Sadie's fall. During the doctor's visit, Sadie's mom also found out about the hoof picking incident and Sadie hitting her head against the stall wall.

"Hi, Dr. Paul, it's Liz Navarro. I hate to bother you again so soon, but I need to talk to you about something else that's happened with Sadie."

"No problem, Mrs. Navarro, please go ahead. That's why I'm here," replied Dr. Paul.

"Thank you, and please, call me Liz. You see, yesterday Sadie's dad left for a deployment to Afghanistan; I think she mentioned that to you when she was there. Anyhow, Sadie came back from the barn, where she had gone to unwind after seeing her dad off, and told me a story about what she is calling an 'encounter.' She seems to think that some horses on the internet need her to save them from an auction, and now she wants to do it." She paused, as if she was hesitating to say the rest.

"Go ahead…," the doctor urged her.

"Well, I need to know if I should be worried or bring Sadie back in for some more tests or something," she said.

"Well Liz, I don't think there is anything medically wrong with Sadie. It's perfectly normal for her to become involved in a fantasy, if in fact it is a fantasy, particularly considering all the stress she's been under with moving, getting ready to start a new school, her dad deploying, and from what I can tell, a rough time training a new horse. She's been through a lot. Besides, many horses at local auctions need help, so whatever she can do for them would be great. Let her be. It can't hurt, and it will give her a good sense of purpose."

"Thank you, Dr. Paul, for your time and counsel. I hopefully won't have to bother you again soon," she concluded.

Mrs. Navarro felt a bit guilty doing this behind

Sadie's back, but she knew it was her job to be the parent, not a friend. She was glad Dr. Paul confirmed her gut feeling, but she would have felt irresponsible if she hadn't checked.

Mom went to Sadie's room, softly shook her awake, kissed her on the forehead, and said, "Sadie, I believe in your new purpose, and I'm here for you all the way."

FREEDOM HILL

Time was running out. Sadie knew she had to move quickly, and she was scrambling for ideas.

It was early October, and November 11th, the day of the auction, was only weeks away. In the two months since the "encounter," she had raised some funds for her mission, but she did not yet have a complete overall plan for saving the ten horses.

When Sadie walked out of school one Thursday, she was surprised to see her mom's car. Sadie's mom was a bit old fashioned and felt that kids should ride the bus, and not be chauffeured to and from school. Two thoughts jumped through her head:

1. I'm in trouble
2. Something bad has happened.

Luckily, she was wrong on both accounts.

"Sadie, you're not going to believe this," her mom began excitedly. "A few weeks ago an old high school friend of mine, Lori Heritage, contacted me on Facebook. We haven't spoken in over twenty years, but we were great friends. You know, I grew up here in Maryland but left after college, so I've lost touch with most folks from here."

"Mom, slow down!" said Sadie, laughing and wondering why her mother was so worked up about an old friend.

"Anyhow," Mrs. Navarro went on, "Lori complimented me on the beautiful horse in my pictures — Lucky. She told me she had a Quarter Horse and did mostly trail riding these days. Then, out of the blue, she told me she has spent most of her time over the past few years on the Board of Directors of a small horse rescue in Calvert County!"

"What?" said Sadie. Did she dare to hope?

Her mom spoke even more quickly, her features animated and full of emotion. After all, while Sadie remained absorbed in her horse saving mission, she knew her mom lived in the real world worrying about Dad in Afghanistan, working full-time, taking care of the family, and being the strong one for everyone. She hadn't felt this kind of spark in some time.

"Through the wonderful technology of the worldwide web," Mom said, "I told Lori about Lucky and your passion for horses, and I asked if you could visit. I also mentioned that you might like to interview the rescue center for a project you were working on, but I didn't say more than that."

That was Sadie's mom. Always helping, but making sure Sadie did the real work.

"Oh my gosh, thank you thank you!" said Sadie, giving her mom a big hug. They talked about the possibilities on the way home.

Sadie immediately went to the barn to see and ride Lucky. "Lucky, I might not be around as much as usual in the next few days because I have to work on a presentation to help us save the horses," she explained. He crunched his carrots, and she was sure she saw a wink of understanding.

Sadie researched horse rescues and found out much more about the "unwanted horse problem." She read that many horses who no longer fulfill their original purpose often end up with owners who don't know what to do with them, or with well-intentioned people who do not have the means to take care of them. Sadly, some greedy people over-breed horses in hopes of making money. Others neglect, abuse, and starve horses, ponies, donkeys, and mules. And, since government subsidized shelters for large animals don't exist in most places, non-profit rescues are often the only hope for survival for these poor creatures.

Since laws in the United States had changed, resulting in a decrease in horse slaughter, horse rescues in the U.S. had been inundated. Sadie was sure that Freedom Hill was no different. Although it appeared cruel to her, the reality was that in the past, horse owners were able to dispose of unwanted horses by selling them at auction to meat markets. Although it seemed crazy, saving horses from slaughter in the U.S. actually increased the number of unwanted horses.

She read on, and learned that sending horses to slaughter in Canada or Mexico was an even worse option, due to the distances the animals have to travel in often deplorable conditions. While international governments were working to find solutions for this difficult situation, non-profit individual horse rescues were busting at the seams with horses that were no longer wanted or could no longer be cared for.

With rescue centers so over populated, Sadie realized she could not just show up and expect any center to take all the horses she needed to save. The fact that she would be presenting a plan, a plan that she thought would work, to a friend of her mom's made it even more difficult. She didn't want to embarrass her mom, or herself.

Another consideration was that Sadie felt an obligation to "her" horses. She couldn't just find them *any* homes; she had to find them good homes. As their only advocate, she knew they depended on her to investigate the rescue organizations or potential homes.

How did I get into this? I'm only twelve! She wasn't sure if she would know what to do if she found a lost puppy, and here she was interviewing organizations to determine if they were suitable to take on unwanted horses?! A wave of anxiety moved through her, but Sadie realized that it was her responsibility, and it was time to get on with it rather than fret.

The Freedom Hill Horse Rescue visit was set for the following Monday, a Federal holiday. Both Sadie and her mom had off from work and school and could go together. Sadie could have scheduled it sooner, driving with Austin, but knew her mom wanted to be there.

Although Sadie had been working on a plan, she hadn't put it into a presentable fashion…or really even thought it all the way through. She took a deep breath and kicked her planning and presentation skills into full gear, starting to pull it together.

When Sadie woke up on Monday, she found a

denim satchel on her dresser that had not been there the night before. A small tag read "Go get 'em girl. Love, Mom." Moved by her mom's thoughtfulness, she unravelled the large cloth bag. Inside, Sadie found a lovely pair of khaki trousers, a button-down collar denim shirt dotted with a horseshoe pattern, a brand new brown belt, and a matching pair of paddock boots still in their box.

As she pulled the paddock boots out, she looked up to see Mom watching. Sadie laughed at the mischievous smile on her mom's face. Her mom gave her a hug, fussed a little and said, "I hope everything fits. You've been growing so fast it's hard to tell these days. I'll leave you to get dressed, but call if you need anything."

Sadie never believed that clothes made the person, which is probably why she was just as comfortable in Austin's hand-me-downs as in anything new. However, as she donned her new "Sadie the Horse Saver" attire, she felt empowered. Viewing her reflection in the mirror, instead of seeing Sadie the barn bum she saw Sadie, the girl with a mission. Even *she* took herself seriously.

As a final touch, she pulled her long wavy hair back behind her ears into a low ponytail and fastened it with a horseshoe clip that Grandma Collins had given her long ago. She'd never found the exact right time to use it, but today seemed perfect. She grabbed her presentation, placed it carefully in her backpack, and met her mom in the kitchen.

As they were about to leave, Austin burst through the door, sweating and out of breath from a hard run. "Sadie," he panted, "I ran as fast as I could so I wouldn't miss you before you left. With every two steps, 'I believe' was pounding in my head. Good luck! I'm behind you all the way!"

Then he stopped and gave Sadie a funny look. "You are my sister, right? Those clothes...."

They all laughed, and Sadie and her mom stepped through the open door.

The two of them followed Lori's directions and finally pulled into a long driveway, lined by horse fences, towards a large yellow Victorian house on the hill. As they arrived, they saw a truck parked by a pasture, and a woman petting a beautiful chestnut horse whose head reached over the fence asking for attention. The woman turned to the car, smiling, and Mom said it was Lori. There were butterflies in Sadie's stomach.

"Lori, this is my daughter, Sadie. And Sadie, this is my old friend, now called Mrs. Heritage." The old friends actually squealed with delight as they greeted one another.

After the introductions and catching up, Lori thanked them for coming and began explaining the horse rescue operation which had been her passion for the past five years. She pointed to two horses in the field.

"See the chestnut Quarter Horse?" She asked. "That's Talutah. We call him Lu for short. He's mine, and my ace trail rider."

Lori pointed to the other horse, a handsome Thoroughbred.

"And that is Lance;" she explained. "He retired from racing a few years back, and Mel, the owner of Freedom Hill, adopted him, giving him a second chance. Shelby, a student from the high school across the street, shares Lance with Mel. She does barn chores and takes care of Lance in exchange for riding privileges."

Lu and Lance were adopted, healthy, and well

cared for; evidence that Freedom Hill was a successful rescue center. Seeing them happily chewing grass in a large green field under sunny blue skies gave Sadie hope. Her butterflies began to settle.

"Freedom Hill Horse Rescue fosters horses at a variety of locations within a few miles of here. Mel stables several of the rescue horses and foals on her property, but the majority of the others live in fields, temporarily donated by land owners. Those of us involved with the rescue center approach local land owners, and ask if they would be willing to lend their pasture for the horses. The property owners benefit by receiving a tax deduction, and they know their land is being put to good use."

"What an ingenious idea," said Sadie, half to herself.

"It does work," replied Lori, "but only because of hard-working and dedicated volunteers."

"What else do the volunteers do?" asked Mrs. Navarro.

"Some spend days getting the fields ready for horses. The horses must have food, water, and shelter. Thankfully, that's now mandated by Maryland law. They also need good fences and pasture without dangerous plants."

"Wow," said Sadie, "that's a lot."

Lori laughed. "That's only the beginning! All pastures need maintenance. Horses love to chew fences and shelters. Fields flood. And sharp objects appear out of nowhere."

Sadie hadn't thought about all these things before. It amazed her that so many people willingly gave their time and effort to help rescued horses.

"Let's climb into my truck and I'll show you the rest of the property," suggested Lori.

"Good idea," said Mrs. Navarro. "Sadie, bring your presentation."

The presentation, thought Sadie. *Yikes*. She realized that her fascination with the rescue operation had temporarily distracted her from her impending meeting. She dutifully tucked her presentation portfolio under her arm and quietly crawled into the back seat of the truck. Lori sensed Sadie's apprehension as she watched her in the rear view mirror, gave her an understanding smile and continued with her tour. Her soothing, melodic voice and warm eye contact calmed Sadie's nerves. She really wished she could just hear about the rescue and forget all about her presentation.

Lori was quiet for a moment. "I'll tell you the story of Nala," she said. "Nala was a little Medicine Hat foal who we sadly had to euthanize. That happens sometimes. We assume responsibility for the horses we rescue, and part of that responsibility is making difficult, life changing decisions when we have to."

"But why...." asked Sadie.

"She was suffering terribly, and the vet said she would be in constant pain for the rest of her life. I know it's sad, but there is another part to this story."

Lori paused before continuing. "It was a beautiful, sunny winter day when we put Nala down, and a group of us were there to comfort her. After the vet arrived and administered the injection, a cold wind came through and flakes of white snow appeared out of nowhere, reminding us all of the tiny foal's distinctive white Medicine Hat markings. The storm cleared as quickly as it came. The sun shone brightly again as if there had never been any wind or snow. And that's the story of Nala," Lori finished.

Lori had spoken with such kindness and compassion for Nala, the little foal. Although the story was a sad one, the caring of those who made Nala's short life worthwhile and comfortable gave Sadie the understanding that this was the kind of place she needed for "her" horses. It was clear from Lori's words that they had done everything they could for Nala. They loved her to the very end, and they still loved her to this day.

That was it. This was the ideal place. Sadie realized she had to put her nerves aside and deliver her presentation with confidence. She had to do it for the horses. While Lori continued to talk about volunteers and feed shifts, and Mom asked a few questions, Sadie ran through her presentation in her mind and talked herself into how easy this was going to be. After all, Lori Heritage did not seem scary at all, and she and Mom had known each other when they weren't much older than Sadie was now. Sadie looked into the rear view mirror again, and Lori caught her eye and smiled once more.

Yup, this was going to be a piece of cake.

ᎏ9ᎏ

PROBLEMS AND SOLUTIONS

Lori slowed down as they pulled up to another farm with a nice big farmhouse, two lovely mares, two miniature horses, and two foals. Lori talked about each of the animals, including Freedom Hill's mascot, Fiona. Fiona stood 9 hands high, or three-feet tall, was black and white, fuzzy like a teddy bear, and had what appeared to be a humped back. Fiona could not be adopted out due to her many medical problems, but her purpose in life was to be an ambassador for the rescue, allow people to pet her, and provide a welcoming "neigh" to the newcomers.

As Lori finished talking about the equine residents of the farm, she turned to Sadie's mom. "I'll call Mel, the founder of Freedom Hill Horse Rescue, and ask her to come down from the house now. Sadie, I understand you have something you wanted to show her?"

Sadie's heart sank, and she stood there with her

mouth gaping open. *What did she mean she'd "call Mel????" Sadie didn't know Mel. Mel hadn't been smiling and making Sadie comfortable for the past hour!* Sadie tried to compose herself. Her mom recognized the awkward silence and came to her rescue.

"Sure, Lori, that would be great. I'll help Sadie get her presentation together, and if it's okay with you, we'll just set it up right here in this picnic area while you call."

Lori answered, "Heck, I'm right here. I'll just walk up to the house and get her. Be right back!" And she smiled again; she had no idea what was going on in Sadie's mind.

But her mom knew. And she had to get Sadie un-rattled before Lori and Mel got back.

"Sadie, this is no different than if you were pre-senting this to Lori. You've done your research on the rescue, and you even read about Mel on the web site be-fore we came here. You have a good, well thought out plan, and these people are taking time to listen to you. Sadie, I believe in you...." she said encouragingly while gently tucking a stray strand of hair behind Sadie's ear.

That was all Sadie needed to hear. Her mom con-tinued talking, but she was no longer listening. Sadie re-peated to herself, "I believe," and remembered that she was here for the horses. She remembered Austin bursting through the door before they left. She remembered that even Lucky believed in her. Somehow, she settled. She was still a self-conscious twelve-year-old doing some-thing beyond her years, but she was also Sadie, who had made up her mind to be a Horse Saver. She was doing what she was supposed to do.

She took a deep breath, and smiled.

"Thanks, Mom," she said before taking her place by her presentation display on a small bistro table facing the three chairs set up across from her.

Lori and Mel walked and talked on their way to the picnic area. Sadie stood with her shoulders back, remembering the way Dad had taught her to stand tall, and tried to look like she was completely at ease standing there. If there was anything awkward about her, Mel didn't seem to notice. Lori introduced everyone. Mel insisted that Sadie call her "Mel," stating she was a horse person, not a schoolteacher, which made Sadie smile. She didn't know whether it was the ease of Mel's demeanor or her great brightly colored rubber boots with pink cartoon running horses on them, but she no longer felt threatened and was ready to get the show on the road. As the women talked, Sadie thought, *Why do they have to chit chat so much?*

"So, Sadie, I understand you have something you want to show us. Would you like to get started?" Mel asked.

Hallelujah. And so she began.

Sadie had organized her presentation into four sections, each with its own graphics. She began with her title slide:

Sadie Navarro's Proposal to Freedom Hill

Calvert County, MD
wealhm@aol.com 443-994-5651

"Good morning. I am Sadie Navarro, and I am here today with a proposal for your organization. I have thoroughly researched Freedom Hill Horse Rescue, and my visit here today reinforces the fact that this is exactly the kind of place that I had in mind for my clients."

At her use of the word "clients," Sadie noticed that both Mel and Lori couldn't help but smile. She also noticed Lori lean over to Mom and mouth the words, "Clients — how cute."

Sadie flipped the stand up presentation folder to begin her next graphic:

The Problem - Unwanted Horses

Hardball: 12-year-old Tennessee Walking Horse cross bred gelding, 16 hands high, bay hunter/jumper and trail horse.

Sunny: 6-year-old American Quarter Horse Mare, 15 hands high, Palomino, basic training.

Sadie began to feel her rhythm, and talked to her audience like she had practiced so many times. She found herself getting excited and speaking quickly, and reminded herself to slow down. She also took a breath, which made her smile. She noticed her audience smile, too, and they all seemed to take another deep breath together.

"I'm aware of the serious nature of the unwanted horse problem, but I don't want to go into specifics because all of you are fully aware of the details and questions surrounding those issues. Instead, I'd like to begin by describing my clients. And by the way, these are not my only clients, but the ones I thought would fit best with Freedom Hill Horse Rescue from what I've leaned from my research.

"I know that rescues are over-burdened and cannot take each case, which is why I offer a cooperative solution." She turned to her next page:

The Solution:

Sponsor Organizations:
Six month sponsorship while re-training and finding homes ($3000.00 each)

The 19th Naval Construction Battalion (Seabees): Hardball

The San Diego Over-70 Surf Club: Sunny

"My plan includes sponsor organizations for the two clients I would like to place in Freedom Hill. My father's group in Afghanistan, the 19th Naval Construction Battalion, began a tiny fund-raising effort and became so popular that they hit the $3000 mark. And my Grandma Collins, with the Over-70 Surf Club in San Diego, not to be outdone by 'a bunch of young folks' matched the contribution. So, at $3000 from each sponsor, I figured that was enough to at least feed, house, and train the horses for their new beginnings.

"I have to confess that each sponsor raised just a little bit more, but I plan to use that extra money to purchase the horses from auction and transport them here. Oh, and a final note, any money Freedom Hill receives from donations to adopt the horses would of course be yours."

Sadie's final graphic was a simple question:

Can we all work together to save these horses?

Yes_____   No_____

Mel put her hands together and said, "Yes, Sadie, the answer is yes."

Sadie had to remind herself to be a young professional and not a kid because what she really wanted to do was jump up and down and scream: "YES!!!!!" However, the women had no such inhibitions. They looked at each other, then stood simultaneously, clapping and cheering for Sadie and "her" horses.

"Thank you, Sadie, for your thoughtful plan. I wish everyone came in so organized," Mel said, while sending an approving nod in the direction of Sadie's mom. "We'll need to work out the specific details down the road. When do you think your – um – clients, might arrive, so I can guarantee a place for them at that time?"

"Mid-November, on Veterans Day."

"Great, that will work. And now, I need to get back to the office - it's always busy here." Just before she turned to leave, Mel said, "Hey Sadie, you did a really good job."

Sadie watched Mel climb the hill to her house and thought, *I just met and talked to a real Horse Saver.* Elated, Sadie and her mom gave each other a huge hug, knowing that Lori was just as excited as they were.

They climbed into Lori's truck and drove to another farm just a few rolling hills away. They saw two wild mustangs Freedom Hill had acquired when another rescue center could no longer care for them. Sadie couldn't believe these were the same horses she viewed on Freedom Hill's web site during her research. These plump, furry, playful mares were a far cry from pictures of half-starved mangy unkempt ponies she had seen.

"We could barely handle these girls when they first arrived. It even took a while to get halters on them. But now, they've been socialized and realize we humans aren't here to hurt them. We are about ready to send them off to be trained, which will help them find new homes," Lori explained.

They next stopped at a farm where four geldings were grazing. The horses looked up curiously as the threesome approached.

"This is Black Jack and Linus, both Tennessee Walking Horses," said Lori.

Sadie couldn't hide her excitement. "I saw them on the web site," she said. "That's why I chose Freedom Hill for Hardball. He's a Tennessee Walker too!"

"That's great," said Lori. "People like the Tennessee Walkers because of their easy dispositions and their gaits, which are smooth for people who have back problems."

They finally arrived back at the Navarros' car. Had it really only been one day? *I've learned so much in so little time,* Sadie thought. She felt a little silly now for being so worked up about presenting at Freedom Hill, but she forgave herself since it was all so new to her. Besides, her mom and Lori had rekindled their friendship, and they vowed to get together soon. Sadie thanked Lori for everything and gave her a small gift she and her mom had picked out. There were goodbyes all around.

And with that, they left.

Sadie talked non-stop most of the trip home. Her mom interjected occasionally, offering helpful advice. She needed to send a follow-up thank you letter to Mel to seal the deal. Sadie knew her mom was right, but she was annoyed anyway, partly because she was tired and twelve, and partly because she could not imagine the people at Freedom Hill changing their minds.

Sadie believed in what had happened today. She pulled out her checklist of "clients", put checks next to Hardball and Sunny, and noted "Freedom Hill" next to them.

Only eight more to go....

❧10❧

THE NEXT STEP

Now that Sadie's first plan had come together, she was ready for her next ventures. Two Thoroughbred horses needed homes, and Sadie planned to ask the Thoroughbred Placement and Rescue, Incorporated, or TPR for short, for assistance. She'd read about TPR in a local newspaper article when she first came to Maryland, and thought they might be helpful in locating homes.

This plan would be tougher than Freedom Hill because she didn't have a connection through her mom. But, at least when she approached TPR she could tell them that she had already placed two horses. That would give her some credibility. When she got home, Sadie thanked her mom for all she had done, and asked if she could go see Lucky to tell him the good news. Sadie did her best thinking on a horse.

"Of course! Go celebrate your success with Lucky. Don't forget your phone so I won't worry. And remember, you can only go on the trail if someone goes with you, even though you might feel pretty confident right now," Mom said with a smile.

Sadie was happy to see her mom so happy. She also knew that she couldn't have done it without her. Sadie quickly changed into her barn clothes, grabbed her phone, and ran back to the barn to tell anyone who would listen that she had found homes for two of the horses.

Typical of a Monday afternoon, the barn was empty, but she slogged through the mud to get Lucky out of the field. While grooming him in his stall, she talked to him, telling the story of the day. She chatted incessantly; Lucky listened well. Behind her, a voice made Sadie jump.

"Wow, I didn't realize how serious you were about all this." It was Jessi.

Uh-oh. She caught me talking to my horse, Sadie thought and felt foolish again. It was par for the course. But, Jessi was a horse person, and horse people understood about talking to horses; she seemed to think nothing of Sadie talking to Lucky. Sadie provided Jessi with a condensed version of the day. She ended by telling Jessi she was now working on the plan for the rest of the horses.

"Tell me a little about the horses you still have to place, Sadie," Jessi said, standing at the stall door and watching Sadie groom. "And you missed the mud behind Lucky's ears. You always want to get that to make sure it doesn't rub his bridle when you ride."

Always teaching, Sadie thought, another reason she liked Jessi so much.

Sadie reached up to brush the mud out of Lucky's mane behind his ears, and he put his head down to help her. She rattled off the remaining horses and each of their situations, and when she got to Thor, Jessi listened intently.

"Tell me more about Thor," she said.

"Well, what I know is that he's a gray 17 hand high, sixteen-year-old draft horse cross who belonged to a girl until she went off to college. The family could not afford to pay for college and the upkeep of such a large pasture pet."

"Did the family try to sell him?"

"Yes, but he is so big, has no formal registration papers, and hasn't been ridden for at least a year. He also has a nasty scar on his front legs from a past accident."

"So they decided to sell him at auction?" Jessi said.

"Yes, hoping someone good would buy him."

Jessi said, "I'll talk to Jan and see if she's interested. We have some larger riders, and we could really use a big, sturdy horse with the right disposition. We had one, Molly, a Shire, and retired her just before you arrived. If Thor needs a little re-training, I'll donate my time. And maybe you can help, too, now that you've learned so much from training Lucky. All right, Sadie, I'm off for a lesson, but I'll let you know what Jan says tomorrow. Bye."

"Bye. And thanks," said Sadie.

Holy cow. Sadie hadn't even thought of looking in her own backyard for a solution for one of the horses. Loftmar already had so many nice horses she couldn't imagine they needed any more. What an ideal solution this would be; she could follow Thor's rescue in person! He might be a superb lesson horse, and he'd flourish with all the love and attention he'd receive at this barn. *Please,*

Miss Jan, believe in Thor!

Sadie went on with her business as if it was every day that she found another home for a horse. She chanted "I believe" to Lucky as she led him to the indoor arena and hopped on. She normally preferred the trail, but she promised she would only go with a partner. Since no one was there, she schooled Lucky indoors, running through the movements with him that she would normally be performing in a riding lesson.

She forced her whirling mind to focus on the Thoroughbreds. As she rode, her plans crystallized. Since her in-person discussions were turning out well, Sadie decided she needed to meet face to face with someone at the TPR. She knew they had a web site, so she'd begin her research there. She had no sponsor organizations for the Thoroughbreds. She knew she needed a different angle.

As she sat astride her amazing horse and felt his beautiful trot, so light and smooth, she thought about how different every horse was. Sadie loved Lucky's trot. Other horses did not have such a great trot. She liked the adorable ponies, but their trots were usually quite bouncy. And while some horses had the most comfortable canter in the world, others had difficulty placing their feet correctly, leading to a very bumpy ride.

Even more than their movement, Sadie marvelled at their different personalities and dispositions. True, many times the treatment they received affected their dispositions, but there were exceptions. Some horses experienced deplorable circumstances and ended up being loving, affectionate animals. Yes, each horse was different.

That's it! It came to her as she and Lucky rounded the next corner at a slow, even-paced canter. She slowed him to a walk so she could really think it through. TPR would take Sadie's horses because she would highlight their uniqueness. She would research as much as she could about each horse and present their portfolios to their new prospective placement service. Since they were Thoroughbreds, they would have records from the breeding and racing association, and she would compile this information to make it easy for the service to place them. *This is the only idea I have at the moment,* she thought, *so I am going for it.*

With this thought, Lucky stopped in the middle of the arena, and Sadie thought it was a good time to dismount and ensure he was cooled down. Riding helped her think, and she now had an answer for her next dilemma. Back in Lucky's stall, she untacked him, groomed him, and gave him a big kiss on his forehead.

She pulled out her phone and pressed number two to speed dial her mom to let her know she'd be home in a few minutes. Lucky nuzzled the phone to make it beep again as he had done so many times. Sadie laughed and Lucky threw his head up and down. Harmony between girl and horse. Sadie headed home. She didn't know how long she'd been riding, but this had been a very, very long day.

The next morning Sadie felt refreshed and ready to tackle the question: Who are the Thoroughbreds? She had briefly "met" Buster and Vixen during the "encounter," but she knew there was more to their stories.

The internet holds a world of knowledge on the horse industry. Sadie began by searching all the web sites she could and any news articles which might contain information on the horses. A master searcher, she came up with information on a "Gray Buster," and knew it was the same horse as Buster.

He was seventeen years old and 16 hands high. His lineage went back to War Admiral, the famous racehorse, and he had a successful show jumping career in Maryland and Virginia. There were show pictures of him in action that she could use for his portfolio. Sadie didn't know what particular circumstances had landed Buster on the auction block, but he had a proven record, still looked good, and would probably still make someone a great horse, even though he was a little old now for his original career as a racehorse.

Okay, thought Sadie. *I have enough information on Buster to convince TPR to rescue and place him.*

Vixen, on the other hand, was another story. Sadie definitely remembered her name, like the reindeer in the Christmas song. She also recalled that Vixen was a 15.3 hand bay filly with a star on her forehead. She was three years old and would give someone years of companionship. More importantly, Sadie remembered that Vixen seemed the most scared, confused, and desperate of all the horses. Sadie could not let this poor filly down.

When she hit a dead end with the internet, Sadie thought she'd talk to the school librarian, Mrs. Hawkins. A lot of kids thought the library was just for getting books out, but Sadie had found throughout her five schools that the library always had answers. Tomorrow she would find out.

Sadie took a break from her project and went to the barn. She had riding lessons on Tuesdays, and although her lesson didn't start for another hour, she had to find an answer on Thor. She had homework, and she knew if Mom or Dad had been home they would have made her finish it before leaving.

"They would understand," she reasoned out loud.

When she got to the barn, there was a note on her locker. She hesitated. This would either make or break her day:

> Sadie, great news! Jan said yes to Thor, and she will pay for him as well. We'll put him in the stall next to Impressive, and you can help me get it ready a few days before he arrives. She offered to let me use the barn's six-horse trailer to pick him up, and any other horses you need transported on the day of the auction. You're doing great!
>
> Jessi.

Is this real? Is this really happening? It made her day.

Sadie pulled out her list again, checked off "Thor," and wrote "Loftmar" next to his name. It seemed unreal. She just needed to believe.

She spent time visiting the horses in the barn and worked on some tricks she'd been teaching Lucky. She saw Jessi walking towards the arena.

"Jessi," she called, "thank you so much for speaking to Miss Jan! I'll thank her too."

Jessi grinned. "Sadie, you have inspired us all. It was my pleasure to help, and I can't wait to meet Thor." Austin walked in as Jessi said, "Now let's get on with your lesson."

She had a fantastic riding lesson, which Austin

videotaped to send to their dad. Sadie thought about training Thor, and realized she'd better really pay attention in her lessons if she was going to help train this gentle giant once he arrived.

After her lesson, Casey asked Sadie if she wanted to go for a quick trail ride. Since Lucky was already tacked up, and she and Casey liked to ride together, Sadie agreed, knowing that Lucky enjoyed his trail excursions. Casey spent a lot of time working at the barn to help pay for her horse's board and her lessons. She seemed to really appreciate her horse. Casey was not much older than Sadie, and Sadie vowed to work at Loftmar as soon as she was thirteen, the minimum age limit for working students at the barn.

Casey's parents restricted her from going on the trail alone, so Casey would only be able to go if Sadie went. *I'm not avoiding homework. I'm helping out a barn mate! It just happens to be fun too!* thought Sadie. They had a wonderful time.

The next day at school, Sadie asked her teacher if she could spend the lunch break at the library. Her teacher, impressed with Sadie's studiousness, checked with Mrs. Hawkins, who said she'd love the company. Most students didn't willingly come to the library during lunch! Mrs. Hawkins listened closely to Sadie's problem with Vixen and began to formulate ideas before she finished. The library had access to a library database, so they could search all Thoroughbred records, not just racing and show results.

"We can also check the Maryland Horse Breeders Association," Mrs. Hawkins suggested, obviously enjoying the chance to help Sadie.

They began searching together, and found Buster

again.

"Look, Sadie," Mrs. Hawkins said, "this isn't great news, but it shows here in the database that Gray Buster's original owners and breeders aren't in business anymore. At least we know."

They still found no trace of Vixen.

Sadie suddenly realized why Vixen's situation saddened her so much. Vixen was probably so scared because she had been moved from place to place and never had a real home with people who cared for her. Sadie knew what it was like to move from place to place.

"Mrs. Hawkins," she said, "we need to find more information somehow."

With Buster it had been so easy. With Vixen, they had nothing except Sadie's memory. She couldn't fake it in her portfolio. She needed more.

Mrs. Hawkins could see Sadie becoming distraught.

"Okay Sadie, we'll switch to the telephone and a live voice. They are great forms of communication and they often work faster and better than the internet," Mrs. Hawkins said.

They looked up the Maryland Horse Breeders Association phone number.

A gentleman answered on the second ring. Mrs. Hawkins put him on speakerphone and explained their predicament.

The man was happy to help and began by explaining that most Thoroughbred horse people conduct due diligence when breeding, buying and training horses.

"The association and most racetracks encourage people to support rescue and adoption efforts and find humane ways of dealing with horses unable to continue racing. In fact," he continued, "most racing associations have anti-slaughter policies, which state that any owners or trainers found directly or indirectly selling horses for slaughter will have their stalls permanently revoked. But, the unfortunate truth is that, although most people believe in retirement, rehabilitation, and if recovery is impossible, humane euthanasia, there are simply some bad apples out there that let greed get in the way of doing the right thing."

He offered a ray of hope. If they were able to get Vixen's Thoroughbred tattoo off her upper inside lip and give it to the association, they could use the identifying information. In many cases the original owners and breeders could be contacted and might purchase the Thoroughbred back, or at the very least ensure that the horse had a good home elsewhere.

"I want to emphasize that *most* people in the Thoroughbred industry want the best for their athletes. But without that tattoo, it's a real long shot, no pun intended, to discover who this filly might be. She could have changed hands several times, or owners could have changed her name, who knows," the gentleman continued.

"Well, thank you for your time, sir," Mrs. Hawkins said, hoping that Sadie would not be too disappointed.

"You're welcome, ma'am, and thank you both for your efforts." They hung up the phone.

Sadie's mind clicked into gear. Now she knew how Vixen was unique. She was a mystery filly. Sadie would tell TPR all she knew about Vixen, and would call in her tattoo the day of the auction. The original owners, breeders, and trainers no longer seemed to care about

Vixen, or she wouldn't be in this situation. She would have to ask TPR if they could give her a temporary home after the auction while her mystery unfolded. Surely they must have seen stories like this in the past. Sadie would just have to convince them that Vixen was worth saving.

Mrs. Hawkins' voice startled her. "I'm so sorry we couldn't solve the puzzle completely, and I'd like to continue to help in any other way I can," Mrs. Hawkins said regretfully.

"Mrs. Hawkins, there's no need to apologize. You've helped me find the answer: Vixen's a Mystery. I can't do anything more about it until the day of the auction," Sadie reasoned. "All of this has helped me formulate my plan, and I'm ready to put together my next presentation. Thank you so much for your time and ideas. I'll come back for more help if I need it – which I probably will."

∽11∾

NEW CAREERS FOR THOROUGHBREDS

Sadie, now experienced from her Freedom Hill visit, contacted TPR through its web site. She drafted an e-mail, edited and approved by her mom, and launched the following:

From: Sadie Navarro <wealhm@aol.com>
To: Ms. Clarke <helpfortbs@gmail.org>
Sent: Oct.13, 2010 5:33 pm
Subject: **Inquiry Regarding Placement Services for Two Special Thoroughbreds**
 Dear Thoroughbred Placement and Rescue, Incorporated,

My name is Sadie Navarro, and I am working to save two very special Thoroughbreds from being sold at auction to potentially unsafe owners and possible slaughter. I have researched your organization and am hoping we can work together to save these two horses. I would like to come visit you and present my proposal. Thank you in advance for your time, and I will follow up with a telephone call in the next few days, unless you'd like to call me first at 443-994-5651. Thank you again, and I look forward to speaking with you.

Sincerely,

Sadie Navarro

Two days passed, and Sadie heard nothing. She was disappointed because she had hoped that TPR might think she was an adult and take her seriously. But, time was ticking away, so she dialed the number on the web site.

"Kim here," was the voice on the other end of the line.

Sadie, in her most adult voice, spoke up, "Good afternoon, ma'am, my name is Sadie Navarro, and I was trying to reach the Thoroughbred Placement and Rescue, Incorporated. Have I reached the right place?" *Ugh – why hadn't she said "person?" It made her sound so young.*

"Sadie Navarro…Sadie Navarro…why, yes, I remember your name now. My, you're quite persistent aren't you?" asked the stranger.

Sadie, not quite sure what to say, and still not sure she'd reached the right "person," said the first thing that came to mind: "Well, they say persistence pays," and let out a faint chuckle.

"I like persistence, Sadie, and even though I get far more requests to place Thoroughbreds than I can possibly handle, I'd like to hear your proposal, since you've been persistent about it. Oh, and yes, by the way, you do have the right place. I am Kimberly Clarke, the founder of TPR. Now I don't mean to be nosey, but does your mom know what you're up to?"

"Yes, ma'am, she's fully aware, and I'll have her speak to you if you'd like," Sadie offered, forgetting to use her grown-up voice this time. It hadn't mattered, since Ms. Clarke figured out quickly that she was young enough to have to check with her mom.

"That's okay, I believe you. I just had to ask. Let's see, it's Friday, and I have a few minutes free tomorrow morning between training rides. Can you make it at 9:00 a.m.?"

"I'll be there, Ms. Clarke, and if it's okay with you, I'll have my brother, Austin, with me."

For a moment, she considered saying that Austin was working with her on this project. Then she had a flashback to Miss Patsy at the Marlboro Horse Ranch and remembered how much she respected her honesty. "You see, I'm not old enough to drive yet, but Austin is, so he helps me get to places I need to go."

"Then I look forward to meeting you and Austin tomorrow morning. Follow the directions on my web site, and when you enter the farm, look for the barns on the left near the cross-country course. I'll be around there. I'm the one with the long brown ponytail — well, the two-legged one with the ponytail," Ms. Clarke said with a small laugh.

Sadie loved the way Ms. Clarke put her at ease, and closed the conversation with, "That sounds good. See you tomorrow, then, ma'am."

Sadie did some additional research on Ms. Clarke. She found a lot of information about her. Kimberly Clarke had dedicated most of her life to her love of Thoroughbreds. For over twenty years, she had been an exercise rider for numerous Thoroughbred racehorse trainers. Just last year, she had founded TPR as a non-profit organization after spending many years finding homes for Thoroughbreds that could no longer race. She was well-respected in the Maryland Thoroughbred community for her efforts and had a reputation for being a persistent, no-nonsense business woman. Sadie couldn't wait to meet her.

Since Sadie's "Horse Saver" clothes had brought her good luck at Freedom Hill, she donned the same outfit Saturday morning. Even though her mom offered to accompany her, Sadie told her she'd be fine with Austin. She knew Mom had very little time off from work, and she felt more confident after her successes so far.

"You can go alone, but I'd love to see a practice run of what you are going to say...like we practiced before your last visit," Mom suggested, as she tucked the tag into the back of Sadie's collar.

"Good idea, Mom," Sadie agreed, and ran through her speech, giving herself another chance to think it through out loud.

Austin piped in. "Sounds good, but we'd better hit the road or you won't be able to say it at all."

Mom offered a few helpful last minute tips without over correcting, and Sadie and Austin were on their way. Sadie practiced what she was going to say one more time in the car. She planned to use the same format she had used at Freedom Hill, but knew she might have to improvise. At least she and Ms. Clarke had a connection. They were both persistent.

Austin and Sadie pulled into TPR's farm at 8:45 a.m. and quickly found the barns and training area. They arrived early and decided to wait in the car for a few minutes so they wouldn't disrupt Ms. Clarke's morning routine. Sadie saw a lean lady with a long brown ponytail and recognized Ms. Clarke from the photos she'd seen while doing her research. Even from a distance, Sadie sensed her tenacity and felt Ms. Clarke would be a new mentor. She was clearly in charge of everything going on in the barn and training area, something both staff and horses understood.

"Okay, Austin, let's go save some horses," Sadie declared.

"Right with you." They left the car and headed for the training area on foot.

Ms. Clarke turned around and greeted them as they approached. "Hi, folks, welcome to our place. Come watch for a few minutes and see what we do here. I'm assuming you are Sadie and Austin?"

"Yes, ma'am, that's who we are, and we'd love to watch. Thank you," Sadie said as they all shook hands.

Ms. Clarke continued to direct activities as she described some of the horses to Sadie and Austin.

"This here is Charlie;" Ms. Clarke said as a gray mare cantered past, "she raced a few years as Charlie's Angel, and brought in over $80,000 in earnings. She got hurt last year and won't race again, but that doesn't mean she still doesn't have a lot to give. This girl's got go, and she can use that willingness and athletic ability as a hunter/jumper, an eventer, a fox hunter, and more. We just need to re-train her for her new job, and she'll do just fine."

Sadie interjected, "She looks persistent," and smiled.

Ms. Clarke looked Sadie in the eye and said, "You've really got moxie, girl. Do you know what that means?"

"Umm...not really, but my guess would be that

it is something like persistent?" responded Sadie.

Ms. Clarke looked back to the field for a moment. "Hey – slow her down, J.C., remember she's not as used to the jumps as you are yet," she yelled to the passing rider, a retired jockey who rode Charlie across the picturesque course with eye-catching custom made jumps. She looked back to Sadie. "Moxie – well, you're sort of right, except moxie, to me, means a bit more courage and determination. And smarts. People can be persistent and not have any of those qualities."

"I like that word then, and I'll add it to my vocabulary," Sadie said, while still watching all the activities in the training area and thinking about sharing her new word with Dad.

Ms. Clarke explained what two of the TPR volunteers were doing in the training area. One was schooling a Thoroughbred to do simple maneuvers such as walking, trotting, halting, and turning, and the other worked with a horse on a longe line that trotted around her in circles. Ms. Clarke explained that racehorses are trained differently than pleasure horses. Many people didn't understand that they needed to be re-schooled once they left the track.

"This unfortunate misunderstanding," she said, "leads a lot of people to believe that former racing Thoroughbreds are bad, when in reality they are doing what we have trained them to do." She also mentioned that she had written an online guide on how to work with off-track Thoroughbreds to help both the horses and the people.

"I know, I read every page of it," said Sadie. "I also know that you don't like the word 'rescue,' because you believe most racehorses do not need rescue, they need new careers."

"You've really done your homework, kid. I like that." Sadie smiled. She hoped it looked grown-up.

Ms. Clarke commended TPR volunteers who did everything from cleaning stalls and feeding to exercising the horses and leading fundraising and public awareness campaigns. J.C., the ex-jockey, had been her partner for years in the racing business, and was her only paid employee. She said, "You may have thought I was short with him. But in this business, when someone's galloping a 1000 pound animal over 25 miles per hour, it's not the time to choose tactful words to get your point across. We've been together long enough that we both understand that.

"So, let's get down to business. What do you have for me, Miss Moxie?" A little startled, Sadie realized she'd said that on purpose. *Boy, do I ever have to deliver now,* she thought. *I have to live up to my new name.*

Sadie fumbled for her presentation and was relieved when Austin stood there in front of her with it ready to go holding it against his chest. He said to Ms. Clarke with his usual easiness, "I don't say much, but I make a very good easel."

Sadie only had three graphics this time. She began by explaining that she was aware of two Thoroughbreds going to auction, and that she thought every horse was unique and deserved a chance. She explained that she had created a profile for each horse for TPR, to give the organization an idea of what they were like. She added that she had researched TPR and thought this would be a perfect place for the horses to be while waiting to be placed in new homes. She briefly mentioned she had already successfully placed three of her ten horse clients, two at Freedom Hill Horse Rescue, and one at Loftmar Stables. She tried not to brag about her achievement, but couldn't help being proud. Besides, she thought it would boost her credibility.

Ms. Clarke listened attentively, as if nothing else was going on in the training area. Sadie asked Austin to flip to the first page of her presentation.

"Gray Buster"

-16 hands high, 17-year-old Thoroughbred gray gelding
-Former racehorse, show jumper, appears completely sound
-Original owners/breeders no longer in business
-Deserves a good home

Sadie began her in depth description of Buster. "I was unable to confirm through tattoo verification that Gray Buster and Buster are the same horse, but unique markings, including a tear in the nostril, point to that conclusion," said Sadie.

She discussed the possibility of original owners or breeders buying back unwanted horses, but that wouldn't be an option in this case because Buster's breeders were no longer in business. Finally, Sadie vouched that Buster would make a fine horse for someone, and if TPR were to take him, he probably wouldn't be there for long. Sadie would even forward all of Buster's pictures and information to TPR for them to place on their web site to help re-home him.

Ms. Clarke just nodded. So, Sadie asked Austin for the next slide, and her "easel" flipped the page to Vixen.

> ## "Vixen"
>
> -15.3 hands high, three-year-old Thoroughbred bay filly with a white star
> -Eyes of a doe, appears very frightened but healthy
> -A mystery, no records found, need tattoo to verify identity
> -Deserves a chance

Sadie unwittingly sped up her speech just like she had at Freedom Hill. At least she was consistent. She caught a look from Austin, slowed down, took a breath, and continued. She just knew that there was *no* reason for Ms. Clarke to take Vixen, and Sadie's ability to save her was going to be based on her next few words. She told Ms. Clarke about her work with the school librarian, and how Vixen, of all the horses she was trying to save, appeared the most desperate.

Sadie was trying not to beg, but she thought it sounded that way. *This isn't going at all like the practice run*, she thought. She finished her discussion of Vixen by stating she was going to get her lip tattoo the day of the auction. Further, since she couldn't rely on the owners, breeders, or trainers, to be available or even be in business, she needed a place to put Vixen until she could figure out officially who she was and who might want her. She hoped TPR could help.

Ms. Clarke nodded again, and Sadie asked Austin for the last page.

> Can we all work together to save Buster and Vixen?
>
> Yes_____   No_____

"And that's it," Sadie concluded, taking another deep breath.

Ms. Clarke looked back over to the training area and saw that everyone was finishing the first half of the morning schedule. She was completely silent for what seemed like an eternity, and then asked Sadie, "How do you plan to get these horses from the auction to here?"

"My mom and I have been looking at several horse transport services. But, it's so expensive, and we don't have much money, so that part of the plan hasn't fully come together yet, to tell you the truth. We have one trailer going, but that won't be enough, there's only room for six of the ten horses."

"I'll go get the Thoroughbreds for you. And you can count on me to transport four more of your clients. Take it as a donation," the veteran horse rider said.

"So, the answer is 'yes'?" Sadie asked, just to ensure she'd heard it right.

"Yes, the answer is 'yes'. You're an incredibly brave and courageous young girl, and you obviously truly believe in what you are doing. We need more people out there like you, Sadie, and the whole world would be a better place. I wouldn't have done this for just anyone, but you're a real winner," Ms. Clarke said with what Sadie felt was true conviction.

Sadie felt her face turning beet red in reaction to these compliments. She managed an awkward, "Thanks.... thank you so much...." and tried as quickly as she could to change the subject. "The auction is on November 11th, and we'll have to be there by 8:00 a.m. I can send you directions and everything else. I can't tell you how grateful I am, and how happy I am that I get to see you again," Sadie regretted saying it as soon as it came out. It sounded so kid-like.

"Thanks, Sadie, and the pleasure will be mine. We'll be in touch. And thank you, too, Austin. I'm very impressed with what you kids are doing. I'd better go now, as we have a lot more 'clients' here on the farm that we need to get working," and she turned to go.

"Wait!" Sadie shouted, just a little too loudly. She pulled the horseshoe hair clip from that Grandma Collins had given her from her hair and handed it to Ms. Clarke. "I'd like you to have this, as a token of our partnership. And because I think you have more moxie than anyone I have ever met. I hope it brings you great luck."

Ms. Clarke looked like she didn't know what to say, and then said, "Thank you, Sadie. I'll make a deal with you. I think you need the luck more than I do right now. On the day of the auction, when you've succeeded in your mission, I'll take the gift then. Deal?"

"Deal," answered Sadie, taking the clip back. She thanked her new mentor again, and she and Austin, who again had helped her through, walked back to the car. Before she got in the car, she turned and gave Austin a big hug and held him for a minute.

"Thanks so much Austin," she said, smiling.

"For what? Being an easel? No problem!"

What a brother, Sadie thought as they laughed.

She looked back and saw Ms. Clarke watching them.

Sadie wondered if Ms. Clarke had a brother, and hoped that she was as lucky as Sadie to have such good people in her life. Once in the car, Sadie pulled out her checklist, checked off Buster and Vixen, wrote "TPR" next to them, and "transport for six horses!" Halfway there... only five more to go....

ॐ12ॐ

SCHOOL AND GRASSROOTS POLITICS

Mr. Edwards made everything fun.

Sadie had never had a teacher like Mr. Edwards, her sixth-grade teacher, who made book characters come alive and got students to work together easily. When their class studied Japan, he erected a large red Torii gate in the classroom. They had just begun studying Kenya, and at the end of the unit he was going to hold a realistic African market with music, arts, crafts, and trading between students. Mr. Edwards rewarded the kids who did their homework and those who were nice to other kids by allowing them quiet reading time in the full-size "reading rowboat" he had docked in the corner of the classroom, surrounded by dozens of plants.

Mr. Edwards had a way of letting kids be kids, but also held them responsible for their own behavior and encouraged them to explore their creativity. He required students to get up and speak in front of the class because it was a skill they would need in life.

Sadie's first classroom speech was, of course, about her horse saving mission. She talked about her trip to Freedom Hill and passed around the presentation she had used. She told them about her research on the Thoroughbreds and shared her success about Thor. She mentioned the remaining five horses she had accepted responsibility for, and the many, many others out there that needed help.

While some students snickered, as eleven and twelve-year-olds sometimes do, Mr. Edwards listened to her with fascination. As he did with so many things in the classroom, he brought the students into the problem, encouraging them to come up with solutions. He asked the class, "So, what else can Sadie do?"

One of the loud mouthed boys in the class smirked, "She can ask the President of the United States to help," which elicited much laughter.

Sadie turned bright pink and wanted to go sit in the rowboat in the corner and hide, but Mr. Edwards easily stepped in to keep the ideas flowing.

"That's a great idea, Patrick, and thank you for volunteering to help with Sadie's project," stated Mr. Edwards, in a way that commanded respect. "However, I think we should start at the Maryland State level before going all the way to the President...just the way we learned right here in class, as you may remember." The classroom laughter shifted from Sadie towards Patrick, and Sadie breathed a sigh of relief. "Let's think as a group and see if we can come up with some good ideas," said Mr. Edwards.

At first, the others were quiet. Finally, one of Sadie's new friends spoke up. Allie McGlade, one of the smartest and friendliest girls in the class suggested, "We could write a letter to our State delegates and senators as a class and have everyone sign it, asking for help for unwanted horses."

Sadie was still standing at the front of the room. Mr. Edwards nodded for her to sit down. "Sadie, thank you for bringing such a pertinent issue into the classroom. I think we're headed for great discussion and an action plan." Sadie sat down and thought that whenever it was that she would start liking boys, she would surely marry one like Mr. Edwards.

For the next fifteen minutes the class worked on drafting a letter to the local Maryland delegates expressing their concern for unwanted horses, suggesting new solutions and providing Sadie's mission as an example of how this affected the Maryland horse industry. By 10:00 a.m. on Wednesday, Sadie had a well-written letter with potentially twenty-five signatures asking for local politicians to help her cause.

Mr. Edwards, whose specialty was social studies, loved to see students exercising their right to freedom of speech and thought this was an excellent demonstration of what he called "grassroots" politics at work. He told the students he would be posting the letter on the class web site that day and needed their parents to approve the students' signatures by the end of the week.

"You all need to understand the importance of speaking up individually and as a group," Mr. Edwards explained. "You each have a voice, just like our founding fathers did, and if you feel an issue is important, it is up to you to speak and be heard!" It sounded a bit dramatic, but when Sadie heard his speech, she felt strongly that what they were doing was right.

Mr. Edwards continued. "Just as important, not everyone or everything can speak for himself, herself, or itself, and so it is up to us to speak out for those who can't," Mr. Edwards said with feeling. Allie had once told Sadie that Mr. Edwards was an actor before he started teaching, and after hearing him, Sadie wondered why he had ever left acting. He had quite a way of convincing people that he meant what he said. But then again, Sadie believed he really was passionate about her cause.

When Mr. Edwards dismissed the class to move on to their math, science, and reading sections, he asked Sadie to stay behind for a minute.

"I hope I didn't embarrass you," he whispered softly so the other kids could not hear.

"No, Mr. Edwards, I mean, I didn't like people laughing at Patrick's comment, but I've learned that if I'm going to do this I have to learn to deal with things that I'm not used to. And I *have* to do this."

The room had cleared so Mr. Edwards spoke in a normal voice. "I know, Sadie, I can see your intensity, and I just explained *why* you have to do it. If you don't, who will?"

Sadie wanted to talk about the people who had been so helpful to her so far, but instead just nodded. She could tell that Mr. Edwards was focused on helping her, the kid who was trying so desperately to pull it all together in a very short period of time.

He walked her to her next class so she didn't get in trouble for being late, and his last words to her were, "Hey, and we're sending this letter to Congress on Friday, with whatever signatures we have the go-ahead for. You can count on me for that, okay?" She nodded again, speechless, that she had gained such tremendous support.

At lunch that day Sadie sought out Allie to thank her for speaking up. Allie shrugged it off as if it were nothing and then introduced Sadie to two of her friends whom Sadie had seen before but not officially met.

"Is there anything else we can do?" one of them asked.

Yes, she thought; *raise money, research the horses on the internet, chase down ten homes, make embarrassing speeches, and be a champion for the horses and find people who will care for them.*

Instead, she just said, "You can make sure one of your parents gives the okay to use your name on the letter by Friday. Oh, and if you feel like it, you can explain the unwanted horse problem to anyone who will listen, because a lot of people don't know about it."

Sadie took a brief moment to reflect. Today her horse saving mission had expanded into a grassroots political campaign. Yesterday, she didn't even know what grassroots meant, and by Friday, she hoped to be sending her letter to Congress. She thought back to her comment to Lauren about Lucky going to Washington, D.C., to be a senator. Maybe she wasn't that far off. She would have to text Lauren and tell her about their latest endeavors; Lauren knew Lucky was special way back when, and wasn't afraid to share that with Sadie.

Mr. Edwards received signature approval from almost all parents, and he and Sadie spent the entire lunch period on Friday e-mailing the letter. Sadie sensed Mr. Edwards had done this kind of thing before. He told Sadie he was going to drop off hard copies at the State Capitol building in Annapolis, on his way home. Sadie knew roughly where Mr. Edwards lived, and figured the

State Capitol was nowhere near his route home. *He must really believe in this cause,* she thought.

Before they even finished e-mailing the letter to their list of delegates, they received a reply e-mail from House Delegate Donna Bragg's office. They decided to finish e-mailing before opening the reply. Sadie's heart was pounding, and Mr. Edwards crossed his fingers. Sadie chanted "I believe" under her breath, and they opened the e-mail together. Surprisingly, Delegate Bragg had herself authored the e-mail, not one of her staff. Sadie read the e-mail:

From: Delegate Donna Bragg
<Donna.Bragg@house.state.md.us>
To: Mr. Edwards <EdwardsJO@pgcps.org>
Sent: Oct.22, 2010 12:36 pm
Subject: **RE: SAVING HORSES**

Dear Mr. Edwards' Class,
I applaud efforts such as yours and would be very interested to talk to you about the unwanted horse issue here in Maryland. I particularly would like to meet the girl who raised the issue and is working on saving particular horses. My calendar is free on Tuesday afternoon, if you can arrange to meet me at my office in the Capitol Building in Annapolis. Thank you, again, and I look forward to meeting you.

Warmest Regards,

Donna

Delegate Donna Bragg
Maryland House of Delegates
Congressional District 23

Mr. Edwards jumped out of his seat, and for a minute Sadie thought he was acting more like one of her classmates than her teacher. He pumped his fist in the air and said, "Yes, yes, this is the way it is SUPPOSED to work!" He then turned around, remembered Sadie was there, and looked a little embarrassed.

Mr. Edwards, back to being the teacher, said, "Sadie, let's strike while the iron is hot. I'll call the office and get a firm time on Delegate Bragg's calendar, and you and I will go. We'll need to do more homework on the unwanted horse problem, but I have a good idea of what to do about that. We'll talk to Delegate Bragg about the overall problem, and then we'll bring the issue to life by explaining what you are doing at the grassroots level. Big picture, and then specific example, right in her own back-yard," Mr. Edwards said with unbridled enthusiasm.

Mr. Edwards shared the good news with the school principal, and Sadie was excused from classes for the rest of the day so they could research and make contacts. One of the social studies teachers took over Mr. Edwards' class so he could devote his time to the project. The first step was easy. Mr. Edwards talked to the delegate's legislative assistant and nailed down a time for 2:00 p.m. on Tuesday. The second step took a little more effort. Mr. Edwards explained to Sadie that almost every organization has some sort of lobbying group, which consists of people supporting an organization's cause. He knew the horse industry had to have one, he just needed to find it.

Using his favorite search engine, Mr. Edwards used the keywords: Maryland, Horse, Associations. Bingo, he found the Maryland Horse Council (MHC). According to its web site, "Since 1983 MHC has represented

Maryland's diverse equestrian community as the horse industry's trade association. We protect and promote the equine industry to the Maryland government and the general public through media and our members." Although Sadie didn't understand a lot of what that meant, Mr. Edwards assured her this meant they were a Maryland horse lobby group.

He dialed several phone numbers until he reached someone in person. Friday afternoon before a Tuesday meeting was not the time to be trading e-mails or leaving voice messages. He reached the current President of the MHC, a well-known local equestrian, and a former grassroots lobbyist himself. Mr. Edwards explained the situation, and the MHC President agreed to send one of his volunteers to accompany them and to answer any questions that were beyond the scope of Sadie's knowledge. He said someone would be in touch with him by Monday, and if he couldn't find someone else to attend, he would attend himself. He ended by saying, "I'm so impressed and excited that a young student and her school are taking such an active stand for the horses."

Preparing Sadie would be the final phase of the project. Mr. Edwards role played with her and asked her questions as if he were a member of Congress. He didn't want her to get caught off guard or have to think too much on her feet, so they rehearsed some potential questions and answers. Mr. Edwards wanted her to be herself, but they both knew a few minutes of extra preparation ahead of time helps in difficult moments. He made it all sound so easy that she felt ready to go immediately.

Sadie spent her weekend doing what she normally did - horses, chores, homework, writing to Dad, and more horses. She texted Lauren with the exciting news, and they now referred to Lucky in their exchanges as "Senator Lucky." She didn't feel that nervous, and she wasn't sure if it was because she didn't completely understand the scope of what she was doing, because the delegate had been so enthusiastic, or because she had already been through two important presentations.

Tuesday would tell.

❧13❧

SPEAKING OUT

When Tuesday morning came, Mrs. Navarro surprised Sadie with a brown suede jacket with fringes to complement her "Sadie the Horse Saver" attire.

"Sadie, you look so good in your new jacket," said her mom. "It's perfect for a visit to an important State Capitol office."

Sadie reached up and felt her horseshoe hair clip. She was glad she still had it. Besides the luck it was bringing, Grandma would get a real kick out of knowing it was worn in a Congressional office. In Grandma's version of the story, it would probably be the lucky hair clip that had gotten Sadie into the office. Who knew, that version may have been right.

"I'll meet you and Mr. Edwards at school at 12:30 sharp," Mom said as she kissed Sadie goodbye.

Mr. Edwards, Mom, and Sadie arrived at the Capitol Building at 1:45 p.m. and met the representative from the Maryland Horse Council in the main lobby. Her name was Stephanie Leonard, and she volunteered on the Legislative and Policy Committee of the Council. Conveniently, her regular job was here at the State Capitol, and she knew her way around the building and its people.

Friendly and down to earth, she told the group, "I'd like to stay out of your way and let you tell your story. I'll mention the Maryland Horse Council and give a brief description of what we do, but the show is yours, Sadie. I'll also step in and bail you out if she asks any questions which I may be better prepared to answer. How does that sound to you? "

Stephanie Leonard is clearly a pro, thought Sadie as she replied, "That sounds great. Thanks."

Sadie understood why Mr. Edwards thought it would be a good idea to have a lobbyist along. The four of them wound their way through the corridors of the historic building, and Sadie tried not to gawk at the detailed rotunda or impressive paintings. She wanted to stay focused, not look like a tourist.

Sadie still wasn't nervous, and Stephanie Leonard put her even more at ease. Ms. Leonard's easy manner and confidence seemed contagious, and Sadie felt it. Plus, Ms. Leonard would step in if need be.

When they arrived at the office, Delegate Bragg's legislative assistant welcomed them, asked each of their names, and asked them to wait while he went to see if Delegate Bragg was ready.

He returned a moment later and escorted them into her office, and introduced each member of the party as if he'd known them for years. Delegate Bragg's smile lit the room, and her presence exuded warmth and charm. She politely greeted everyone and then zeroed in on Sadie.

"It is such a pleasure to meet you, Miss Sadie. I've so been looking forward to it because you and I have something in common."

"We do?" asked Sadie, sounding surprised.

Delegate Bragg laughed. "Yes, we do! You see, when I was about your age, I found out about the wild mustang round-ups out West. They would round up the wild horses for slaughter because there were too many of them. I thought this was terribly cruel and unnecessary, and that there had to be a better way. So I wrote whatever congressmen and senators I thought would listen, and told them what I thought. I never got an answer, and I don't know if I made a difference back then. I do know that they stopped the practice for years," finished the charismatic politician.

"No one answered your letters?" asked Sadie.

"No," said Delegate Bragg. "That's why I was so quick to respond to you."

"Thank you," Sadie said. "Helping the horses is really important to me."

"Then let's hear your presentation," said the delegate.

Following the template Mr. Edwards laid out for her, Sadie talked about her internet research and the growing issue of unwanted horses. After providing an overall scope of the problem, she narrowed it down to her specific story. So far, Mr. Edwards' planning was right on target.

Delegate Bragg kept stopping and asking Sadie questions. She could answer all of them, but was afraid it was taking too long. She looked to Mr. Edwards, who gave her the "everything is fine" look and then to Ms.

Leonard, who couldn't be smiling any brighter. So, she relaxed and continued, and ended with, "I now have just a few days to find homes for the last five horses and ponies, which is what I need to get back to just as soon as we leave here."

"Wait a minute," Delegate Bragg said, "you mean to tell me that this story is ongoing? I didn't understand that; I thought it was finished." It was the first time Sadie had seen the delegate's glare, and she was glad it was aimed at the legislative assistant and not her. He looked back and shrugged both shoulders and shook his head. "You mean to tell me you still have horses waiting to be adopted?"

"Yes, ma'am, and if you'd like, I can tell you about each of them. I don't need a script or notes or anything to do that. I know these horses and ponies like the back of my hand. Let me start with Lucy and Ricky. They are two grade ponies - which means mixed breed, or people don't know what breed they are. But I can guarantee you, ma'am, they are the cutest ponies and have the kindest eyes, and they didn't do anything to deserve being sold at auction."

"I understand that, Sadie, and you can stop there. I will take one of the ponies – put me down for Lucy – like the old television show, right?"

"Um, well, yes ma'am, but you see the problem is they come as a pair. They've never been separated, and it would be devastating to split them up now, particularly after all they've been through," Sadie said innocently, unaware that she may be pushing it. To her, she was just being truthful about her clients. She was also a little in shock that the delegate was actually providing a home.

"Well then, I will adopt both Lucy and Ricky, and

provide them a good home. We can't break up the pair, right? After all, in the TV show, what would Lucy have been without Ricky? Or Ricky without Lucy? We live on a big family farm, and my sister used to have horses. With a few updates, I'm sure we'll have a cozy home for the ponies. My kids have been bugging me to get a pony, and between them, the rest of the family, and other kids who come to the farm, those ponies will get plenty of love and good use. I may not know if my letters affected the fate of the mustangs many years ago, but I know I can make a difference for these ponies today."

She finished with, "And Sadie, I want you to know that *you* made a difference today."

Before Sadie could respond, the delegate's legislative assistant pointed at his watch, and Delegate Bragg said, "Yes, I know I have another appointment. Can you please go tell them I'll be with them in a minute? Thank you." And he left. She continued, "So does anyone else have anything they'd like to say before we adjourn?"

Mr. Edwards said, "Thank you so very much for your time, ma'am. This has been such a valuable lesson, and we'll be sure to report back to the rest of the class what happened here today. And thank you, too, for helping Sadie with her cause. Our entire class believes in what she is doing, and she is really working hard to make this happen."

She shook his hand, thanked him for bringing the issue to her attention, and handed him a small glass pen and pencil holder etched with the State Congressional seal. Sadie knew he would cherish it. "Thank YOU, Mr. Edwards, for being such an outstanding teacher, and making sure these young folks know that they do have voices that can be heard." *Wow, just like he said,* Sadie thought.

The poised Ms. Leonard handed Delegate Bragg a small package about the Maryland Horse Council, and said, "The Maryland Horse Council is here to serve you, and the people of Maryland. Please do not hesitate to call if there is anything we can do or any questions we can answer." And with a smile, "You might want to keep those numbers handy with your new ponies inbound." They all laughed.

Sadie's mom hadn't said anything, so the delegate took the opportunity to compliment her on her daughter, and said she knew how important good parenting is. Sadie's mom thanked her, and the entire crew took their leave. They bade farewell to Ms. Leonard, and got in the car.

"Good job, again, Sadie," stated Mom.

"Good job – unbelievable job, you mean!" exclaimed Mr. Edwards. He really did get excited about these things. "You walked in there to increase awareness about an issue of interest to you, and you walked out with her being a true believer! Not only that, but you found homes for two more of your ponies, which was almost only for one of your ponies, until you convinced her otherwise."

And they all laughed again.

Sadie sat back deep in the backseat. She pulled her list out of her bag, checked off Lucy and Ricky and wrote "Delegate Bragg" next to them. Three more to go....

❧14❧

MEDIA POWER

Allie McGlade's mother was a news reporter for *Capitol News*, one of the local Washington, D.C., television stations. Sadie thought that was pretty neat, and she enjoyed watching Allie's mom show up in interesting places on the early morning news. During her breakfast before she left for school, Sadie regularly watched Diana McGlade braving the early morning hours and weather, reporting on large traffic back-ups, upcoming exciting events like parades, and human interest stories.

Mrs. McGlade covered every story with enthusiasm no matter what it was about, and viewers were faithful to her show. It didn't hurt that Mrs. McGlade also had that movie star quality that kept people glued to the TV no matter what she said. Sadie had to admit she was a little jealous of the beautiful reporter.

But Sadie's jealousy went out the window when Mrs. McGlade called Sadie's mom to talk about her horse saving mission.

"I believe people would be very interested in hearing about Sadie's cause, and particularly what she is doing as a twelve-year-old," Mrs. McGlade told Sadie's mom.

Would she approve of Sadie's story airing on the news? Would Sadie be interested in a live interview? Sadie could be a little shy, but could overcome her shyness to help save the horses. Sadie and her mom agreed the interview would be a good thing to do. *I have to thank Allie for this,* thought Sadie. She had taken to heart Sadie's request to talk to people about the unwanted horse problem.

Mrs. McGlade thought having horses in the scene would make for better television coverage, and since Sadie could not get to the horses she was saving, Mrs. McGlade suggested they use Lucky; it really was just for visual purposes. Miss Jan thankfully gave the okay for the photo shoot on her property.

So, at 5:00 a.m. on Thursday, a television news truck pulled up to Loftmar Stables. Sadie and her mom were waiting, and Lucky was as clean and polished as he'd ever been. Lucky looked carefully at the news cameras, as they were clearly things he hadn't seen before. But, in his usual nature, once he realized that these people and equipment were safe, he turned back to the hay bag Sadie had hung for him outside to help keep him happy despite the commotion.

Sadie had never met Mrs. McGlade in person before and marvelled at how she was actually prettier in person than on TV. She was also very kind. When she spoke to Sadie, she made her feel like she was the most important person in the world. Mrs. McGlade asked her a few questions, made some notes on her pad, discussed the physical layout of the shoot with her crew, and then said, "Okay, let's roll 'em."

It was all happening so fast that Sadie didn't have time to get nervous. Her mom was in the background and gave her the "thumbs up" signal and a wink. That made Sadie smile; Mom knew it was Dad's special signal for her. So, with Mom there to support her, Dad there in spirit, and Lucky standing next to her, Sadie knew it was going to be fine. Just then, as if on cue, Austin appeared at the top of the hill and Lucky let out a small whinny as if to say, *Okay, we can start now – everyone is here!*

Sadie and Lucky stood together, with a nice green pasture behind them to set the scene. One of the television crewmembers clacked two attached striped boards together and announced, "Horse kid, take one."

The cameraman zoomed in on Mrs. McGlade as she began to report the story.

"We are here at Loftmar Stables this morning in Bowie, Maryland, with a very special girl on a very special mission, and with her, her horse helper, Lucky. You see, Sadie Navarro has taken it upon herself to save ten horses that may otherwise be bound for slaughter if she does not find them homes." She turned to Sadie. "So, Sadie, tell our viewers about your horse saving mission."

Now the camera panned over to Sadie and to Lucky, and she began to feel nervous. To calm her nerves, she began to pet Lucky, and traced his "I believe" markings, all while trying to remember what Mrs. McGlade had said. Right. Tell the viewers about the mission. *Here goes.*

"Well, it wasn't something I really set out to do, it just kind of happened. I had been looking at horses for sale on the internet, and my dad had asked me to look into horse auctions because he thought we could get a good deal. And then one day, I was showing Lucky some of the horses I could have gotten instead of him, and we came upon a scene of ten horses to be sold at auction. Then something happened that I really can't explain."

"Go ahead and try, Sadie," coaxed Mrs. McGlade, in a voice that made Sadie feel important, not like a nervous twelve-year-old "horse kid."

"Somehow Lucky and I can communicate, and somehow we bonded with the horses waiting to be sold at auction. I don't know how. But anyway, I ended up finding out that these horses are good horses and ponies and they really just need a second chance. So that's what I am doing, trying to give these horses a second chance. Some of them no longer can be successful in their original careers, but that doesn't mean they don't have a purpose in life. We want to help these horses find their new homes and careers. If they were people, we wouldn't throw them away."

"You are so right, Sadie, and this is such a noble cause that you have taken on at your young age. Now, can you show me how you can communicate with Lucky?" Mrs. McGlade asked.

Huh?! They hadn't discussed this in the pre-interview. Did she seriously think Sadie could make Lucky talk? Now what was she supposed to do? She thought quickly, and remembered a horse trick she had taught Lucky.

"Lucky, how many horses do we have left to save?" Off screen from the TV cameras Sadie tapped her foot one, two, and three times, with Lucky repeating each one, while the camera zoomed in on his tapping hoof.

She patted him on his neck, and he nuzzled her. *Whew, she thought, good going Lucky!*

"That's great, Sadie. Now, is there anything else you would like to share with our audience?" *A much better question than the last,* thought Sadie.

"Thank you, Mrs. McGlade, yes there is something I would like to share. As Lucky just said, we still have three horses that we need to find homes for by next week. One is a large draft horse named Goliath who used to pull a carriage. He is as sweet as can be and could do many jobs. Another is an Appaloosa, Spot, who was a parade horse and would make a wonderful trail horse. And last but not least is an Arabian whose name is Chance, who can no longer be ridden, but would make a great companion for anyone who wants to share life with a very sweet horse," Sadie finished.

"So," Mrs. McGlade reported, "all of you out there heard this very special girl. She needs help with these last three horses. Please call the number at the bottom of this screen, or go to our web site for the link "Sadie Saving Horses" if you think you can help. Monetary donations will be accepted as well, since Sadie still needs to purchase and transport all these horses from the auction. All ten of these horses deserve a chance to find their new purpose in life, and thanks to Sadie and Lucky, they are getting that chance. I'm Diana McGlade, with *Capitol News.*"

It was a wrap. No take two. By 5:30 a.m., Sadie had completed her first television interview.

Truthfully, she just wanted to forget about it. The stupid horse trick would make her look like an idiot, but she'd had to think fast, and that's what she'd come up with. Oh well, maybe they would edit out some of the story and just keep in the important part, like how to contact Sadie and her mom in case anyone watching at 7:00 a.m. happened to be shopping for horses. Sadie tried to shrug it off and remember that all of this was for the horses. Besides, she was sure they would be moving again before long, so she would only have to be humiliated for about three years.

The crew packed up the gear, and Mrs. McGlade thanked Sadie, Mrs. Navarro, and Austin for their time. The TV crew was in a hurry because they didn't have much time before this segment showed on air. When the truck drove off, Sadie put Lucky back in his stall and hugged him for being such a good sport.

The Navarro family walked back to their house. Mrs. Navarro made breakfast, and she and Austin talked the whole time about what a good job Sadie had done. After Sadie complained about the stupid trick, Austin disagreed. "I think it will catch people's attention." He turned out to be right....

On the *Capitol News* station at 7:00 a.m. the telecast began. At 7:15 came the teaser from Mrs. McGlade, "And stay tuned to hear about a very special horse saving girl right here in our neighborhood."

A commercial break, and there was Mrs. McGlade again, looking just like she had this morning at the stables. Sadie watched, waiting for the edits. There were none.

Somehow the magic of TV cameras and angles made it all come together nicely. Sadie ordinarily felt self conscious about the way she looked, but she didn't mind the way she came across on TV. She looked more like a normal young girl than like a tall skinny kid.

And, Lucky looked magnificent! The white, or

"chrome" on his coat glistened in the morning sun. His expressive eyes came across beautiful and inviting. When he tossed his head, his black-and-white mane shone and flowed like hair in the movies. Sadie couldn't help but burst with pride! He seemed to love the camera, and no one could have trained a horse to look more lovingly at its owner than the way Lucky looked at Sadie. The cameraman really earned his pay check in the way he shot and edited the counting trick because it looked like they had practiced it to perfection.

Sadie was surprisingly excited about her television debut. The story was short and visually appealing. Mrs. McGlade made it sound like the most important news story of the day, and Lucky performed like a champion. Now they would have to wait and see if it would yield results.

Sadie and Austin went off to school as if it were any other day, and Mom left for work. *Maybe no one in my class watches the news,* Sadie hoped. Even though the story was pretty good, she did not want to be the center of attention.

When Sadie got to school, she was relieved to find that her celebrity status was not a big deal. Her classmates were used to Allie's mom being on TV all the time, and the fact Sadie had been on the news with her didn't faze anyone. And, it turned out that most of her class didn't watch the news at 7:00 a.m., so most weren't even aware of the interview.

At 10:00 a.m., the school secretary, Mrs. Thornton, sent a note asking Sadie to come to the school office. When Sadie arrived, Mrs. Thornton handed her a note that said, "Please call Mrs. McGlade – URGENT!" The secretary dialed the number for her and handed her the phone.

As Sadie listened to the voice on the other end of the phone, a look of shock crossed her face.

"What is it Sadie?" Mrs. Thornton asked, unable to handle the suspense.

"Mrs. McGlade said there has been an overwhelming response to the news story this morning on the unwanted horses. They already have volunteers to provide homes for all three of the horses and donations are pouring in. She wanted to let me know right away. All I can say is WOW!" Since she was at school, she decided she could finally act her age. She jumped up and down, hugged Mrs. Thornton and said, "YESSSSSSS!" in her most twelve-year-old voice.

Sadie returned to class, feeling a little stunned.

She had done it. They had done it. She would need to find out more to ensure the last three horses went to good homes, but she felt such an intense sense of relief, like she could relax for the first time since this all had started.

****

Three hours earlier and fifteen miles away, two men, a big one and a skinny one, watched the morning news. They groused over coffee, complaining about runny eggs to the big one's wife, who had cooked them.

"Hey, look at 'dis," said the bigger of the two, pointing to the TV. "Dis little goil has a pretty looking hoise. I wonder how much that kinda pretty is worth. Plus," he snickered, "look at dis. The goil says dat he can communicate." They both laughed.

"Hmmm…dat could come in handy, huh?" the

skinny one said with a dark look on his face. "Maybe we could get 'em and see how much we can get for him. Jack up North is lookin' fer a flashy pinto just like dat fer one of his hoity toity high dollar customers. Said he'd pay good money fer da right look. We could use da cash, it's been a good long time since we sold a good one or one of our nags has won us anything on the track."

"Yous don't usually say too much smaht, ya moron, but whacha just said makes some sense. Da hoise showed he can count, so he hasta be smaht, too," reasoned the big one.

"Well maybe we could borrow him," the skinny one said with a wink, " and see if we can sell him. We got da contacts to do it."

The wife piped in, "And his name is Lucky, how oh, so convenient, you bunch of Sherlock Holmes's." She rolled her eyes. "But you can't really be serious. You really gonna go steal a little girl's horse?"

"Shuddup, you, you ain't got any beddah ideas, do yous? Dis was just about given ta us. We know da barn he's at and what he looks like." The big one said, in a low voice, as if someone would hear him. "I say we goes and scope da place out, and see how easy it would be."

"This is too much," said the woman. "I can't listen to this."

Ignoring her, they devised a plan to take their trailer and park in the landscaping company's driveway adjacent to Loftmar Stables, and walk on foot through the riding trail in the back. All they had to do was pull Lucky out of his stall and sneak him away, leaving the stall door open so it looked like he just escaped. They'd see if they could get a decent price for him, and if they couldn't, they'd decide what to do with him later. A simple plan, and if they got caught in the act, they would claim they just wanted to see the celebrity horse – no ill intentions. Sure.

Sunday would be a good day to do a dry run, just as the sun was setting. The barn would probably be empty.

"Hey," the skinny one said, again with a sickening snicker in his voice, "and maybe this psychic communicating hoise can tell which of our nags has injuries that won't never heal, and which ones is lazy. Or which of them mares will give us winning foals."

The big one laughed and slapped the table with his hand. "That ain't a bad idea. That ain't a bad idea at all. We might as well try while he's here, I guess."

Through it all, they never saw the woman walk out the back door with her suitcase.

Their luck was indeed about to change.

৵15৶

VICTORY RIDE

Sadie called *Capitol News* when she got home from school and spoke with the receptionist, Lupe, who was collecting information about viewers who wanted to help the horses. Sadie thanked her and said, "It's so important to find good homes for the horses."

"Good luck," said Lupe as she gave Sadie the contact information of three volunteers so she could interview them. "By the way, the online donations have already reached $1050, and people have until midnight on November 8th to donate," Lupe informed her. "In my experience, most donations come in just after a story airs, so they will probably taper off at this point."

Sadie was floored. "I hadn't even thought of online donations! Mrs. McGlade did so much. This is all completely bonus – a much-appreciated bonus."

Sadie dialed the first number on her list. It was a therapeutic riding center. She spoke to a woman named

Marilyn who wanted to adopt Goliath. Marilyn had been with the center for years and said that Goliath sounded like the perfect therapeutic riding horse.

"We've just taken on the mission of helping wounded warriors recover from battlefield injuries, which we believe is providing a much needed service to our nation's heroes," Marilyn explained. "We need some larger, calm horses to help those with special needs. I'd like to invite you out here for a tour, and show you how we use the horses."

"Thank you for the offer, ma'am, but I only have a few days left to find homes for the horses, and I can't think about much more than that right now. But, I really look forward to meeting you and seeing Goliath in his new home. It sounds like such a perfect match!"

Sadie dialed the second number and was amazed when she got a live voice again.

"Prince George's County Mounted Police unit, Sergeant Lucero speaking," reported the voice on the line. Sadie didn't even know that her county had a mounted police unit!

After Sadie introduced herself, Sergeant Lucero told her, "We are a very small unit, but are beginning to grow. Spot's experience as a parade horse gives him a good foundation for mounted police work, as he should already be used to crowds and loud noises. I also happen to have a real soft spot for Appaloosas, since my first horse as a kid was an Appy," confessed the Sergeant.

He gave Sadie the link to their web site to show that they were very legitimate, invited her to visit, and even gave her his personal cell phone number. Sadie knew she had found Spot's home.

It struck Sadie as interesting that everyone was so

friendly to her, and guessed it must be because they felt they knew her from her TV appearance. She wondered if people treated Mrs. McGlade the same way, and if so, why everyone wouldn't want to be a news reporter. She dialed the final number, hoping to find a good home for Chance.

A familiar voice answered the phone, "Hello, Marlboro Horse Ranch."

"Miss Patsy! It's Sadie Navarro, and...."

"I know! I saw you on TV and remembered you immediately. You and that handsome, quiet brother of yours. One of my boarders here, Sue, had two horses that were together for years at the ranch. One of the pair just died of old age at 34. The horse left behind, Occhi, has been depressed and lonely ever since. I recommended Sue adopt Chance to be Occhi's new companion. Sue doesn't ride anymore, hasn't for years, but loves horses, and jumped at the idea of saving Chance and to make Occhi, and herself, happy again."

The last home was found.

****

Sadie had five days left to finalize the plans. She still had to figure out finances, coordinate trailer transport times with Jessi and Ms. Clarke, and contact the other new horse owners to confirm delivery times.

Right now, all she wanted to do was go for a victory ride on Lucky to celebrate their success. There were a few hours of daylight left, and she was going to use that light doing what she loved best – trail riding. The ride would help clear her mind and help her solve any last minute issues. It had been a long day and she was tired.

She figured she deserved a break. Off she went, cell phone in hand, hoping that someone else would be at the barn who would want to go for a trail ride.

As she walked down the gravel road to the stable, one of the boarders, Camie, drove up. Camie rolled down her window and jokingly asked if she wanted a lift, since the barn was about fifty feet away.

"No thanks," Sadie laughed, "but would you like to go on a trail ride? I want to go on a victory ride because we just found homes for the last horses. I can't think of a better way to celebrate."

"You did?" exclaimed Camie, "That's great! I am supposed to be schooling Blue for the upcoming hunter/jumper shows. But why not, we can go on a short trail ride and then practice. I wouldn't want to miss a victory ride."

Sadie admired Camie, one of the best riders at the barn. She worked so hard, stayed focused, and although in her twenties, never treated the kids differently from anyone else. Camie owned Blue, the 17 hand high dappled gray Dutch Warmblood, who was one of the most beautiful horses Sadie had ever seen, and Lucky's first buddy at the barn.

They tacked up their horses and headed out on the trail, with Lucky leading the way and Blue close behind. The two horses were buddies in the field, and were very comfortable on the trail together. Camie and Sadie talked about horses, school, and other trail rides they had been on in other places. The crisp fall day was beautiful and Sadie soaked in the colors changing in the trees. A small herd of deer scampered off in the distance and the horses reacted only slightly. Deer were abundant in the area, and the horses were used to them so they didn't spook. They just tensed their muscles a bit.

Sadie realized she wasn't doing much thinking about the auction and decided to ask Camie if she had any ideas.

"Well, I've never been to a horse auction, but it seems like key ingredients would be halters and lead ropes, hay and water, money and trailers, and people in the right places at the right times," Camie said, thoughtfully.

Sadie had thought of all those things, except for having people in the right places. It was a good point. Sadie couldn't be bidding on the horses, taking them to trailers, keeping track of the auction schedule, and paying all at the same time. She would have to assign people roles. It may have seemed simple, but it was key to the operation.

They took the short route back to the barn, which was fine with Sadie because Camie had been kind enough to go on the trail when she had training to do. Although she never mentioned it, Camie had probably figured out that Sadie wasn't allowed on the trail by herself.

Before Sadie dismounted, Camie asked her for a high-five exclaiming, "Here's to the victory ride!"

Sadie brought Lucky into the barn, and Camie rode into the outdoor arena to start schooling with Blue. Sadie realized again how lucky she was to have met so many good people here in Maryland, a place she was sure she was going to hate just a few months before.

❧16❧

MISUNDERSTANDING
COMMUNICATION

Sadie spent much of Saturday laying out her plan for the auction and adding up her auction money to determine how much she could spend on each horse. It was a difficult task, because this would be a live auction with no set prices. When deciding which people should be in which positions, she knew her mom had to be in charge of finances. As an accountant and a math whiz, she was most suited for the role. Sadie also knew that whoever was handling the money would have to be close by her, and as much as Sadie might be growing up, she really wanted her mom close by her throughout the auction.

Between sponsor organization donations, the *Capitol News* station's online fundraising drive, solicitations from her barn, the local tack and feed stores, and a fundraising booth she and Austin had set up outside the local grocery store, Sadie had raised $11,876. Six thousand dollars of that total she promised to Freedom Hill to maintain two of the horses during their re-training, so that left $5876 to purchase ten horses. Sadie spoke to an equine appraiser, and asked her opinion on how much she thought the horses would cost at auction.

"You can expect to pay between $50 and $1000 for each horse, depending on the bidding," the appraiser said. Sadie hoped to buy a lot more $50 horses than $1000 horses.

On Sunday she took a break from her chores and auction planning, and went to the barn, hoping for a trail ride. There was no one else at the barn when she arrived, so she took as long as she possibly could grooming Lucky, hoping someone else would show up to ride with her. It wasn't a particularly pretty day, a bit gloomy actually. But the air was crisp, the leaves were falling, and it still seemed to be a day for the outdoors.

When no one else showed up at the barn, Sadie rode Lucky in the outdoor arena, schooled him over small jumps, and worked on her equitation skills. She thought back to her first day on Lucky when the big blue heron had swooped down, and realized how far they had come together. Perhaps because there were no other riders in the barn, Sadie felt a tinge of loneliness, and was relieved that she had her best friend, Lucky, right there.

After dismounting, Sadie reasoned that it would be safe if she took Lucky for a walk on the trail, leading him instead of riding him. It made sense to her. She had never done it before, but then again she had never thought of it before. She set out on foot and the uneven footing gave her a new appreciation for the abilities of trail horses. After catching a branch or two in the face she wondered why horses didn't put up more of a fuss, and started paying closer attention to what was ahead of her.

Too stubborn to turn around, Sadie forged ahead in the thick mud and tried to enjoy the serenity of the woods.

The trail looked quite different on foot than it did atop her big horse. She followed what she thought was the right path and ended up surrounded by holly trees and sticker bushes, clearly in the wrong place. Lucky looked at her as if to say *"I told you it was the other way,"* and she couldn't help but laugh.

"I'll listen to you at the next fork in the road," she said, and hugged his neck. They got back on track and descended deeper into the woods; the sounds of deer in the distance were muffled by the leaves rustling as the wind picked up.

Sadie thought she heard a car door shut and found that odd. They were far out in the woods, and she'd never heard anything like that before back here. She chalked it up to her imagination, or a branch breaking, and put her mind back to navigating the roots and rocks on the trail and avoiding the branches that came at her face. Then it began to rain.

It wasn't a drizzle; it was a downpour. Sadie still hadn't quite figured out this Maryland weather. It seemed like it could be bright and sunny one minute, pouring rain the next, and then bright and sunny again. It hadn't been a nice day, but she hadn't expected this! Sadie couldn't see two feet in front of her face. A thunder clap came from above, as loud as she'd ever heard and she thought it shook the earth. Lucky pulled back on the reins, but considering the sound of the thunder, he behaved well.

Sadie stood still and comforted Lucky, at the same time comforting herself. She looked to see if there was any shelter under which they could hide from the storm, but she couldn't see anything. Then she remembered seeing an old abandoned deer stand on the trail. Sadie was pretty sure it was only a few hundred yards from where they stood and set out to find it, leading the way for Lucky. The sky darkened even more, rain pelted them, and the wind howled. Sadie regretted going out on the trail alone now.

Another clap of thunder shook their ears, and Sadie looked back to ensure Lucky was okay. His eyes were wide, his nostrils flared, but he looked at Sadie as if he trusted her. Sadie continued forward, picking up the pace because she wasn't sure how long Lucky could keep his cool. Thinking she was on a familiar path, she turned back to Lucky to calm him and tell him they were almost there. By the time she faced forward again, it was too late. She plunged down a deep ravine and into a stream at the bottom with a loud splash and a scream.

Lucky's instincts to flee from danger took over. Sadie had let the reins go during her fall. Lucky took off in a terrified gallop through the woods.

Sadie could not afford to feel pain or panic. She had to get a hold of herself quickly. She pulled herself out from the mud, climbed up the ravine, and called after Lucky.

It was useless. He was well out of her earshot, and the rain and thunder were too loud. Horses instinctively return to their homes, and Sadie hoped that Lucky was on his way back to the barn. She didn't blame him for being so scared and losing his confidence in her.

Sadie went for her cell phone to let somebody know what was happening. This was no longer about her stubbornness or pride, it was about making sure Lucky was safe. Of course, her cell phone was safely tucked into her saddle bag – on Lucky. She took a deep breath, told herself that was okay, and that everyone would find out soon enough what was going on when Lucky came galloping up the path to the barn alone. As a source of strength she said out loud, "I believe you're going to know what to do, Lucky," and trudged back towards the barn, paying very close attention to where she was going this time.

****

Less than a mile away, two men could not believe their eyes. Standing in front of them through the pelting rain in the woods was the tri-color pinto they had seen on TV. He was breathing hard and pawing the ground. They looked at each other, smiled, and the big one said, "I told ya it wuz a good idea ta come taday." And they both snickered sinisterly.

"Heah hoisey," said the skinny one. "Come ta papa." He moved closer to Lucky.

Lucky didn't trust these strangers, but, scared and exhausted, he let the two men approach. The big man took hold of Lucky's broken reins and yanked him hard on the mouth. Unaccustomed to this kind of treatment, Lucky reared to get away. As his front hooves returned to the ground, the skinny man smacked Lucky hard enough on his nose with a log so that he saw stars. Dazed, frightened, and exhausted, Lucky gave up and followed the pull of the reins.

"Lookey heah – now we don' even hafta go to da barn to get him. I told ya, dis was supposed ta happen fer us," said the big one.

They led Lucky to their trailer, parked out of sight

at the business next door. Now, as fate would have it, they were in an even better position. A horse wearing a saddle out in the woods alone indicated an accident had happened. The people at Loftmar would think he was lost somewhere rather than stolen. As they drove away they agreed that their luck was already changing.

They never gave a thought to the missing rider.

❧17❧

TROUBLE CALLS

Sadie ran the last half-mile to the barn. The rain had subsided a little but showed no signs of stopping. Looking for hoof prints on the trail was useless; it was so sloppy it was impossible to tell what was new or old. She hoped to see Lucky grazing in one of the pastures as she approached the barn.

Nothing.

She looked in the barn hoping to see him standing in the aisle way, wondering why someone hadn't opened his stall door for him yet.

Nothing.

She looked in the indoor arena hoping maybe he had found his way in and was drying off and relaxing.

Nothing.

No riding lessons took place on Sundays, and the barn was empty. With the rain, it was doubtful anyone would be coming out to ride. The barn workers would be there at some point, but Sadie needed help right now. And she was all alone.

She missed her dad terribly and knew that if he were here he could somehow make everything right. She tried not to think about how much she missed him at most times, but right now she couldn't help it. Somehow it seemed unfair that the only person who could make everything better was on the other side of the world helping other people instead.

Although she'd never done it before, she knocked on Miss Jan's door out of desperation. Miss Jan answered the door, looked Sadie up and down and asked, "What on earth happened to you?"

Sadie spoke 100 miles per hour telling Miss Jan the story, trying not to get too emotional about it. It didn't work. Through tears and sobs, she explained that she scared Lucky, and he ran away, and it was all her fault, and she'd never go on the trail alone again, and that she didn't deserve to have such a wonderful horse, and she didn't blame him if he never came back.

Miss Jan, with three daughters of her own and having had years of experience dealing with horse-crazy kids, knew exactly what to say. She told Sadie to calm down, that Lucky would be fine, and that everyone would do whatever they could to get him back. Miss Jan said she'd let the workers and neighbors know what happened and call animal control.

"I'll keep an eye out for now," Miss Jan told her. "You run home, get into dry clothes, and tell your mom and Austin what happened. And, don't be so hard on yourself. It was a simple mistake, but surely one you'll learn from."

She reminded Sadie about horses' instincts and

uncanny memories of knowing how to make it back to where they are fed. Even though Sadie wasn't any closer to finding Lucky now than she had been before, she felt just a tiny bit better.

Both Mom and Austin were home, and they listened while she explained what had happened. When she was done, her mom said they'd work on a plan while Sadie got cleaned up.

"I don't need to get cleaned up! I need to go find Lucky!" she argued. But she lost that battle.

When she returned in dry clothes, her mom and Austin were waiting in their rain gear with flashlights in hand. Austin had quickly put together a flyer with Lucky's picture and the words: LOST, please return to Loftmar Stables or call 443-994-5651. Their plan was to post the flyers, grab buckets of grain from the barn, and head out onto the trail to look for Lucky.

Sadie led the way down the trail. Soaked in mud in minutes, she wanted to ask again why she needed to get cleaned up for this, but thought better of it. After all, the only reason everyone was out here was because of her stupid mistake, and her mom hadn't even mentioned the fact that Sadie had disobeyed her.

The threesome shook soggy buckets of grain calling "Lucky, here Lucky," and looked for clues. After three laps of the trail in each direction, the weary, wet group returned to the barn to see if he'd turned up.

Nothing.

The dark day turned to dark night, and Sadie's spirits grew darker as well. The barn workers pitched in to help and took turns patrolling the trail to see if Lucky had wandered back. When the flashlights could no longer penetrate the darkness, and there had been a few too many stumbles, the search party decided to wait until morning to resume the search.

"Please, Mom, let me keep looking," Sadie pleaded through tears.

"No, Sadie, it's too dangerous for everyone," her mom answered firmly.

"Hey, I'll camp out in the barn all night in a sleeping bag to see if he shows up," Austin volunteered. "Maybe Lucky's afraid of all the commotion and voices. Maybe once things quiet down, he'll come back."

Sadie liked that idea and asked if she could stay too, but knew better than to push it when her mom said "No, Sadie, you've had enough excitement for one day."

Sadie tried to sleep, but couldn't. She e-mailed her dad not knowing what time it was in Afghanistan, but hoping he would answer. Before long the phone rang, and it was him. This was one of the few times she had heard his voice in months, since phone calls were only allowed in emergencies. Lucky's disappearance, or more appropriately, the effect that his disappearance had on his daughter, counted as an emergency.

"Everything's going to be all right, sweetheart," Dad said, sounding so far away.

"But it's dark out there, and he doesn't know where he is, and this is all my fault. I have no idea what to do, Dad. I'm so scared."

"Try to believe that everything is going to be all right, and that you'll find him as soon as it's light out," he said in that calm, soothing voice. "Keep the faith, Punkin. He's going to come looking for you." Sadie wanted to believe him with all her heart. When they said goodbye and hung up the phone, she cried and cried, missing her dad more than ever.

She eventually drifted off to sleep, only to have a nightmare of Lucky running through a dark forest of finger-branches reaching out to grab him. He was covered in mud, and the finger branches kept scratching at him, making him bleed. The more they grabbed, the more scared he became, and the faster he ran. He turned back, desperately looking for Sadie to save him, and fell into a deep ravine, rolling and rolling head over hooves.

She bolted straight up in bed, covered in sweat.

The rest of the night Sadie tossed and turned but could not fall back asleep. She wanted so badly to sneak back to the barn and wait for Lucky with Austin. But, she'd gotten into this mess by making up her own rules, and reconsidered.

She tried to focus on anything other than worry. She imagined Lucky grazing happily in a neighboring pasture, alongside the cows, wondering why they didn't look, sound, or smell like him. She tried to think of the auction, but that made her even more anxious. Lucky had to come back; there was no way she could pull off saving the horses two days from now without him.

Light through the windows made Sadie open her eyes, and she realized she had fallen asleep at some point. Austin hadn't come home, so she knew Lucky hadn't returned. Mrs. Navarro took the day off of work and kept Sadie and Austin home from school. She and Sadie headed for the barn to relieve Austin from his duty and to continue the search. The rain had stopped, but it was windy and cold. They retraced the steps they'd taken yesterday over and over and looked for any clues revealing Lucky's whereabouts.

Nothing.

They drove up and down to the road to see if

somehow Lucky had made his way onto one of the neighboring properties. They brought their flyers and tacked them to telephone poles, fences, and trees on all sides of the Loftmar property. Mrs. Navarro's cell phone rang, and it was the county animal control, saying they received Miss Jan's report. They wanted to confirm with Sadie that they knew Lucky was missing and would be on the lookout. Mrs. Navarro thanked them and impressed upon them how important it was to find him, and soon.

After searching all morning they returned to the house with Austin to brainstorm more, sitting around the kitchen table. If they were horses, where would they go? They sat in silence, each in their own thoughts, when the cell phone rang again. Sadie hoped with all hope that it was the county animal control office or Miss Jan calling to say they had found Lucky.

But it wasn't.

Mom answered the phone, but soon had a very puzzled look on her face. She didn't say anything, just put her phone on speaker and placed it in the middle of the table for Sadie and Austin to hear.

"Well lookey heah, the hoise wants ta use da phone," cracked a voice from the cell phone. "Ain't dat funny. Who ya gonna call, Lucky?" and a big-bellied laugh followed.

"Hey, maybe dat's how he communicates – get it?" And another town idiot laugh bellowed.

Sadie knew those voices, and a chill ran up her spine as she remembered a pasture full of starving horses, and a big black truck blocking their way. She started to say something, and Austin quickly hit the mute button on the phone. He gave her the "shhhh" sign with his index finger and continued to listen intently. The men obviously had no idea that Lucky, playing with the phone, had pushed the speed dial button. In the background, Sadie heard Lucky's unmistakable whinny and heard him pawing hard at the ground.

"Hey, it looks like dis phone is woiking, Tommy. Hang it up, ya dummy. We don't need ta be calling some strangjah ta let 'em know about our talkin' hoise," and more laughter. Sadie wanted to scream; she saw nothing funny about this. And then the phone went dead.

Mom stared at the phone with eyes as wide as Lucky's in the storm. Austin and Sadie looked at each other and knew right away they had heard those voices before: the thugs at Jake and Tom's Stables. Austin did the talking because he could speak much more sensibly than Sadie at this point.

"Mom, remember the day we went looking at stables, and we told you about a barn that had dirty pastures and sad horses and some pretty mean guys? Well, we didn't tell you and Dad how bad those guys really were because we didn't want Dad to go over there or call the police. We were trying to be mature. We didn't think we'd ever see or hear from these guys again. But we just did."

Sadie's mind was spinning. She figured it out immediately. Jake and Tom, obviously some kind of horse gangsters, had seen Lucky during her television interview and for some reason had stolen him. *Do they literally think he can communicate with them?* she thought. She couldn't figure out exactly how they'd stolen him, but it probably had something to do with his escape on Sunday. Who knew what they wanted with Lucky. What was going to happen to Lucky when these awful people couldn't get what they wanted out of him? *I'm such an idiot*, she thought, and she felt sick at the thought of her horse at the hands of Jake and Tom.

She thought about how often she and Lucky played with the cell phone, and how he liked to make it "Beep." She thought it was funny at the time. She never thought it would actually work like this.

Lucky must have nosed the phone and hit the speed dial button. It pained her to know that Lucky had no way of knowing that they had heard him.

Mom still looked overwhelmed, so Austin suggested a simple course of action. "I think we need to call the police," he said, with a voice of authority far beyond his sixteen years.

"You're right, Austin. I'll do that right now. They must be able to help," Mom said. "This isn't good, but at least we know Lucky is…well, alive." It hit Sadie that her mom had even considered Lucky might not be alive and she put her head in her hands, sobbing. Austin put his hand on her shoulder.

Mom phoned the police and explained the situation, with Austin and Sadie listening to one side of the conversation. It didn't sound good. The horse had called? And the kids think they recognized the voices from a brief meeting they had in a driveway four months ago? The police said they would file a report, but there wasn't enough evidence for them to do anything. Sadie got the impression that Lucky's disappearance was not high on their list of priorities.

Sadie had to think fast, something she'd been doing a lot lately. They could not just go to Jake and Tom's Stables and demand Lucky back. Sadie was not too stubborn to admit she was afraid of them.

Then it came to her. The mounted police – they would understand. Sadie thought about her conversation with Sergeant Lucero of the Prince George's County Mounted Police, how nice he had been, and how he had given her his personal cell phone number.

Sadie dug out Sergeant Lucero's number and called him. She left a voice-mail that she needed to speak to him on an urgent matter.

An hour later the phone rang. "Sergeant Lucero here – is something wrong with Spot?" he asked.

"No," Sadie answered, "but something terrible has happened to Lucky." She explained the whole situation, and he listened to every word.

Sadie let her mom talk to Sergeant Lucero, and they agreed that it would be better if he just came over so they could all talk in person.

Sadie paced by the front door, waiting for him to arrive. She knew he would be there soon and didn't want to seem ungrateful for his help, but she sure wished he'd hurry up.

Sergeant Lucero showed up in a sedan, not on horseback. He took a lot of notes and did not seem skeptical at all that Lucky could have been abducted by Jake and Tom. Sadie explained how Lucky liked to play with the phone, and of course the fact that he was very special.

"I saw him on TV and could see that he is special," Sergeant Lucero said. Sadie got a lump in her throat.

Working this county his entire life, Sergeant Lucero knew of Jake and Tom's Stables. He, and others in the horse industry, knew their operation was shady, but the two cousins somehow avoided getting caught breaking the law. It was within the mounted police's jurisdiction to drop in on Jake and Tom's stable to ensure they were in compliance with Maryland stable regulations regarding food, water, shelter, and adequate veterinary care for their horses. He did not need probable cause to do so at any time. It was part of his job.

A beat detective for years before becoming a mounted police officer, Sergeant Lucero was well qualified to plan the rescue of Lucky. He radioed his team, and Sadie, Mom, and Austin listened as the plan unfolded.

Jake and Tom knew it would look suspicious if they had Lucky, so they would be on the lookout for any vehicles that didn't regularly visit. They probably figured they had a few days before anyone would investigate their place, since Lucky had disappeared in the woods.

Sergeant Lucero congratulated Sadie on her junior detective skills and for figuring out that they probably had seen Lucky on TV. At this point, the way Jake and Tom had abducted Lucky wasn't so important; getting him back was.

Because Jake and Tom would be on the lookout for vehicles, Sergeant Lucero and two of his deputies would enter the property on horseback, quietly, at night. Lucky would have to be in one of the indoor stalls, because even Jake and Tom knew that to leave him outside would be too risky. There was only one barn with indoor stalls on the property, but they would have to make it through several pastures full of horses, and past the house, before getting to that barn. If the horses on the property nickered when the police horses arrived, things could get tricky. Then again, horses nickering on barn property wasn't such an unusual occurrence.

Understanding there was no time to waste, Sergeant Lucero said "OPERATION RESCUE LUCKY" would mobilize that night.

"I need to go now to arrange all the logistics and

brief my crew on the plan," Sergeant Lucero said. "I have a great team who will be dedicated to getting Lucky back." he assured them. "I'll call the minute we have Lucky in hand." He looked at Sadie. "It's going to be fine."

Amid all the chaos, Sadie once again felt extreme gratitude and felt very blessed to have met such wonderful people along her way to saving horses. As she watched Sergeant Lucero pull away, Sadie softly mumbled, "I wish we could be there tonight," and turned to look at her mom, expecting a lecture on safety.

Instead, Mrs. Navarro looked deeply into her daughter's eyes, and knew that all Sadie wanted in the whole world at that moment was to go and save her horse. She pondered, and the wheels started turning in her mind.

❧18❧

OPERATION RESCUE WATCH

Sadie waited.

"Well, Sadie," Mom finally spoke, "no one has told us that we CAN'T be there. Sergeant Lucero didn't exactly keep the details a secret - he planned it right in front of us. I mean, we can at least go and watch what happens." Sadie saw the same twinkle that had been in her mom's eye when she first told Sadie about Lori and Freedom Hill.

Sadie was a little shocked. She had just watched her play-by-the-rules mom turn into this daring detective. Her spirits began to lift. Unaware of the surprise in her voice, she asked, "Okay, Mom, so what's your plan?"

Hearing the tone in Sadie's voice, Mrs. Navarro laughed. "You two may think I'm just a boring accountant!" she said. "Someday I'll tell you about our reputation in your dad's squadron earlier in his career. Nothing illegal. Just some scheming, sneaking around, pulling pranks on the higher ups. One time we accidentally put the base on red alert.... but that's for when you kids are older."

Austin and Sadie were staring at their mom, mouths open. Actually, her impromptu revelation had both distracted and settled the three of them.

Sadie broke the silence. "I've never thought you were a boring accountant, Mom."

Her mom laughed. It was Austin who brought them back to the task at hand.

"So Mom, what's your sneaky not-quite-illegal plan for tonight?"

"Let's see what the three of us can come up with. We're a team."

The three of them sat at the table, where not long before they had received the most important clue to Lucky's whereabouts. Mom started listing all the facts: the who, what, when, where, and why. Their purpose was not to save Lucky; the mounted police would take care of that. Their purpose was to observe OPERATION RESCUE LUCKY and not get in the way.

They seriously considered the circumstances and decided that, although it probably wasn't the brightest thing for them to be doing, it wasn't as if they were walking into a shoot-out. Jake and Tom appeared to be bumbling crooks, not murderers. Or so they convinced themselves.

"I have one major rule here, team," Mom said. "We will not get close enough to put ourselves in danger. We have to keep our distance. I haven't completely lost my mind." She sounded a bit more like the mom they normally knew.

Their plan, named OPERATION RESCUE WATCH, began to take shape. The mounted police would conduct OPERATION RESCUE LUCKY on horse-back later in the night at Jake and Tom's Stables, with the action likely to take place at the house or barn.

"So," Mom said, "let's talk about the EEI..."

"Wait," Sadie said. "What is EEI?"

"EEI means Essential Elements of Information," Mom explained. "It's the facts that we need to know to carry out our operation."

What else don't we know about our mom, thought Sadie.

They sat and thought for a moment. The "who, what, and why" of the plan were obvious.

"I've got an idea for how to figure out 'where,' and I'm going to do some work on the computer," said Austin. "I think you'll be just fine without me for a few minutes," and he went to the den. As usual, he was the calm in the storm.

Mom and Sadie worked on the "when." Anx-iously looking at the clock on the wall they realized that time was passing by and they'd better figure it out fast. It would be dark in a few hours. The rescue would take place somewhere between 7:00 p.m. and 5:30 a.m.; a pretty big window. The longer they stayed in their "watch" spot, the better the chances of being found, or even worse, of foiling the rescue operation. They had to narrow the time down.

Calling the police to ask what time to show up wasn't an option. There had to be another way to figure it out. Sadie wracked her brain, listening to the radio that Austin had on in the den. In a flash, it came to her.

"I've got it! The Police Band on the radio! You know how we've always teased Dad about his goofy hobby of listening to the different radio bands? Finally it's not so goofy!"

"Sadie, that's an excellent idea!" said her mom. "And thank goodness I even know how to use it. I don't know why I didn't think of that earlier. It was never really my thing, but your dad did show me how to dial it up and taught me some codes. I know he didn't take that radio with him to Afghanistan. This is great! We can listen to the Police Band and figure out when the team is headed out for the operation. Keep this up, Sadie, and one day you'll be as good of a sleuth as me," she said, smiling.

Austin walked in with pages of photos and a grin that said he'd figured out the "where." He laid the photos out on the planning table and grabbed a pencil to use as a pointer. It looked like something out of the old war movies. Austin had found and printed satellite maps of Jake and Tom's property, which showed the fields, the house, the barn, and the roads in. He never ceased to amaze them.

"Here is the road Sadie and I used when we went to Jake and Tom's back in the summer," Austin stated, as if in a military briefing room. "And here is another road to get to the barn from the opposite side of the farm. I'm sure Sergeant Lucero and the deputies will enter the farm from the route Sadie and I took, since we talked about that when he was here. The back road, from the images, looks to be completely passable, and I even found a way we can get there from the main roads. It figures that guys like this would have a "getaway" road.

"I propose we come through the back road and park on the far side of this broken down barn and position ourselves behind this clump of bushes. We should be far enough out of the way to steer clear of danger,

Mom, but still meet the objectives of OPERATION RES-CUE WATCH," Austin finished, with his pointer pencil still in hand.

Either Austin had been watching too many war movies or had a natural inkling for military or police planning. Whatever it was, Sadie was surely grateful for it at the moment.

Mrs. Navarro paused and looked reflective for a moment.

"What are you thinking, Mom?" asked Austin.

"Oh," she said, "I was just thinking about your dad's early Navy days again. We used to have these excellent road rallies, which are kind of like scavenger hunts with cars. It took a lot of teamwork for us to win those, and it struck me just now as we are planning all of this that we are a great team." She looked back at Austin's satellite maps. "Now lets get back to it."

The police would probably try to conduct the operation when Jake and Tom were asleep, to have the element of surprise. That would probably be sometime after 11:00 p.m., which meant the watch team needed to be close to the scene around that time. They would wait at a location slightly off the property, and listen to the Police Band. When the mounted police unit moved into position, they would move to their watch location. Once there, they would be absolutely silent and not move, staying hidden from the view of the house and the indoor barn but able to see the action.

All three would dress in dark clothes to stay camouflaged at night, and carry three things: a flashlight, a cell phone, and a whistle. The whistles were for protection in case they needed to signal each other quickly. Austin would hold their one pair of binoculars to keep a close eye on the events as they unfolded. When the mounted police had the culprits under their control, the watch team would appear from behind the barn and the bushes and announce their presence to the police. Then, Sadie would go to Lucky and make sure he was okay.

At Mom's urging, the watch team began to look for holes in their plan and better ways to accomplish the mission. They decided to bring some hamburger meat to appease any dogs that may come after them, and turned their cell phones to vibrate to ensure they wouldn't be given away by a phone call. With an eye on the clock again, Sadie realized it was time to mobilize.

Sadie jumped at a knock at the door, and all three froze. Austin quickly picked up his images and Mom shoved their planning notes and lists into a drawer. Who could it be? Had someone heard them planning?

Mom slowly and cautiously went to the door, and looked back to ensure the room was clear of planning evidence before she opened it a crack.

"Heeellllooo, love!"

Sadie squealed with delight as she realized it was Grandma Collins! She jumped to the door, which was now open wide, and gave her grandma the biggest, strongest hug ever.

"You didn't think I could just sit there in California and do nothing while my poor granddaughter was looking for her horse, did you? I'm here to help. Now let's get to work," she said, not at all weary from her cross-county airplane flight.

Sadie and Mom exchanged glances, which Grandma Collins quickly deciphered as meaning something between "uh-oh," and "oops." Although this had all happened so fast, they realized they had forgotten to call Grandma Collins to tell her they had found Lucky. Even if they had called, Sadie reasoned, she wouldn't have picked up the message on her cell until she was in the taxi from the airport.

"Mom," Mrs. Navarro began, apologetically, "there's something we need to tell you, you see…"

Sadie burst in, "It's my fault we forgot to tell you, Grandma, and I'm sorry. We've just been so busy planning OPERATION RESCUE WATCH that we didn't think to call, and…"

"Girls, I have no idea what you are talking about," Grandma Collins said. "Austin, can you please tell your poor grandma what's going on here?"

"Sure. The police know where Lucky is, and they're going to rescue him tonight. We're going to watch, but we can't let the police know we're going to be there, because they'd tell us not to be there. And we need to get moving, now, or we're going to miss the whole thing."

"Why so blue, then? This is fantastic news! I'm so excited to be here to help. You heard Austin, let's get moving!"

Mom said, "Okay, let's get your bag in the spare bedroom and start looking for some dark clothes for you. Austin, go round up another flashlight and whistle. We know Grandma has a cell phone. Bring all the planning papers and pictures with us, and you explain the details to Grandma in the car. Sadie,…" She turned around to see that Sadie had already left to get ready.

⧼19⧽

COPS AND
ROBBERS

Within a half-hour, everyone was ready to go. Grandma made the brilliant suggestion that they bring along some sandwiches because somewhere in the excitement of planning, everyone had forgotten to eat. Grandma didn't think they needed noisy tummies rumbling to give away their position.

It was so wonderful to have her along. Sadie already imagined Grandma Collins telling this story in the future. They packed the car, ensured they had the GPS and maps, and tried to act nonchalant as they pulled away.

An abandoned store's parking lot just off Jake and Tom's property served as their waiting point. Sadie's mom was pretty good at reconnoitering, and at precisely 10:45 p.m., the voices on the police band revealed that the mounted police were on their way. Between Mom's memory of Police Band jargon and Dad's cheat sheet taped to the radio, they were able to de-code the talk that probably sounded like gibberish to others.

They began to slowly drive towards their watch location. The night and stillness were eerie. But the landmarks were easy to spot, and Mrs. Navarro vectored them into the exact location they had decided upon. She told them to close their eyes for thirty seconds, then open them, and their eyes would quickly adjust. Even with the moonlight, it was a dark night. Sadie's admiration for her mom was growing by the second

Before they left the car, Mom turned to Grandma Collins and ordered, "Now remember, no talking!" Sadie could see the surprised look on Grandma Collins' face, and it reminded her that simple words can have a lasting effect.

Sadie tried to make light of the moment and said, "But we can sure talk about it later!" It was a feeble attempt, but at least made Grandma smile. Besides, Grandma knew her daughter very well and realized she was taking her role as "commander" of this operation seriously.

Ever so quietly they opened the car doors and crept out, ensuring they weren't stepping on any branches. Austin's scouting paid off, and their watch spot could not have been any better, with a perfect view of the house on the left, the road in the middle, and the barn on the right. They were sure not to miss anything.

They stayed quiet and motionless for what seemed like hours, and Sadie held her watch up to the moonlight to see they had been in place for fifteen whole minutes. As she looked forward again, she could make out some figures in the distance.

Austin tapped Mom on the shoulder and passed

her the binoculars. Sadie nodded to Austin that she had seen, and Mom passed the binoculars to Grandma. Grandma passed the binoculars back, and held up three fingers to signal that there were three mounted police.

Sadie marvelled at how silently the police moved in. They were riding just off the road in the soft grass to mask the horses' hoof steps. No horses nickered, and no dogs barked. The loudest noises Sadie could hear were the beating of her own heart and the breathing of her team. She took a deep breath and thought, "I believe."

As the mounted police approached the house, Sadie heard Lucky's unmistakable whinny. It sounded so sad and so desperate that she wanted to forget about all the objectives of this stupid OPERATION RESCUE WATCH and run down and help him. Her mom's head snapped in her direction with a *don't-you-dare* look, and Sadie collected herself. She knew she needed to be patient and let the police do their job, but it wasn't easy.

Suddenly, the door to the house flung open, and a big sounding voice hollered, "Hey, ya stupid UN-Lucky hoise, doncha know we's tryin' ta sleep heah?"

The big man, Tom, cocked his head as if he'd heard something else. He looked in the direction of the noise and saw Sergeant Lucero fifty yards to his left. Tom instantly ran out the door and bolted down the hill away from Sergeant Lucero at a surprising pace. Sergeant Lucero motioned for his two deputies to enter the house, and took off after Tom.

Tom headed strait for the watch team. Sadie could hear wheezing and panting as he zigged and zagged toward them. He had the small advantage of knowing the terrain and was likely headed for the "getaway route." Austin stayed motionless with his binoculars trained on the approaching man. With his free hand, he held up a "stop" signal to tell the watch team not to move.

Please stop, please stop, Sadie prayed. All this planning and detective work had been fun until it struck her hard and fast that they were in danger. That awful heavy breathing was so close. She tried to freeze every muscle in her body so she didn't move....but she had to see what Mom, Grandma, and Austin were doing. She glanced over, and they were frozen as well. The second she looked back, she met his eyes only a few feet away.

Those same bushy eyebrows and dark eyes she'd seen months ago were boring into hers. He seemed to pause for a millisecond of recognition and sheer disbelief. Then he lunged forward to grab Sadie or anyone else, and let out a raspy snarl. Sadie closed her eyes and readied herself for the blow.

Sergeant Lucero's horse closed the gap at a full gallop. He dismounted before his horse came to a halt, landing on both feet, still unaware of the watch team's presence. In one quick motion he had the crook's hands behind his back and handcuffed. How he did that with one hand while using his other to cover Tom's mouth was something Sadie would never figure out. She realized he covered Tom's mouth so he wouldn't alert any accomplices on the property.

"Not a word out of you," Sergeant Lucero said to his prisoner as he escorted him down the hill. His police horse dutifully followed.

By the time Sergeant Lucero and Tom reached the house, the two deputies emerged with Jake, handcuffed and dragging his feet, and claiming he had nothing to do with whatever was going on. The house was now empty.

Not surprising, Sadie thought, *who would want to be with these creeps?*

A police cruiser pulled up, and the police loaded Jake and Tom in the back, with Tom shouting, "The goil, I saw the goil over there. She's gonna be sorry! You're all gonna be sorry!"

The cruiser drove away with lights flashing. Sadie hoped this was the same disinterested police team that had filed their report a few hours ago, completely skeptical of her story.

The watch team saw that the police had the criminals in custody, and all appeared safe. Mrs. Navarro stepped out and blew her whistle, and quickly followed with, "Don't shoot!"

Geez. Sadie hadn't even considered that if they made an unexpected noise, the police might think they were more bad guys. She understood now why her mom had been so insistent about staying quiet, particularly with her normally chatty Grandma.

The brightest lights Sadie had ever seen were in her face, and it hurt her eyes. "Who's out there?" a voice she didn't recognize shouted.

And then she heard, "Sadie?" from a voice she did recognize, Sergeant Lucero.

"Yes, it's me…and my mom, and my brother, and my Grandma," she said sheepishly, standing with her hands up in the air, flashlight at her feet.

"Stay put," he ordered, and she could tell he was not happy. Sergeant Lucero mounted and rode closer.

"I'm not going to lecture you, Sadie, about how stupid and dangerous this was for you to be here. But YOU," he said, pointing to Sadie's mom, "You should know better."

"I do know better, but my daughter needed to be with her horse, and right now he needs her. Thank you for all you have done. My daughter would really like to see her horse now, and I'm hoping you will help us make that happen, now that the situation is safe."

He looked at her, astonished at her calm manner, and apparently not knowing what to say. With the lights still glaring, he finally spoke.

"I think I see now where Sadie gets some of her courage. Follow me, let's go see Lucky." The four of them trundled down the small hill to the barn following the sergeant, who was still on horseback.

When they were within scent distance, Lucky started whinnying non-stop. The two deputies had freed him from his stall, and he was standing in the barn aisle. When Sadie came around the corner and he saw her, he broke away from the deputies and ran to her. He instantly calmed and dropped his head when she touched him. Sadie burst into tears, threw her arms around his neck, and buried her head in his shoulder. She told him she loved him more than anything and was so sorry. The tears were both sad and happy, and she didn't care who was watching.

He looked terrible, as though he hadn't eaten or drunk for days, but she was just happy he was all right. The family joined her, and they each gave Lucky a pat, forgetting for the moment that the police weren't happy with them.

Sergeant Lucero told them he had to take Lucky to the county mounted police stables for the rest of the night and complete some paperwork. He assured them their veterinarian would look at him in the morning. Sadie apologized for Lucky's whinny as the mounted police unit approached the house.

"No need to apologize," Sergeant Lucero said. "It brought Tom out of the house and allowed us to move in. Lucky gave us probable cause to believe he was there and helped make this operation a success."

"Of course he knew what he was doing," Grandma Collins had to add. "Don't you know this is a special horse?"

Jake and Tom were on their way to jail for stealing Lucky. Sadie thought back to when she had first seen the horses at their property and had hoped that one day she could help them. This wasn't the way she'd imagined it, but she was glad she had contributed all the same. She hoped that Sergeant Lucero and his crew received adequate credit and accolades for their bravery and dedication.

****

When Lucky arrived at Loftmar the next morning, he still looked beat. Sadie had never seen him look worse, with his coat caked in mud, eyes listless, wobbly legs, and scratched body. As he walked off the mounted police trailer, Sadie thought he looked at her almost apologetically. He nudged her towards his stall, walked in, lay down, and immediately let out a long, relaxed snort. Sergeant Lucero told her that their veterinarian had given him a clean bill of health, but said he needed lots of rest, hay and water.

Miss Jan gave Lucky lots of hay and water, and it appeared he was enjoying resting. Sadie wanted to clean him up and stay with him all day, but her mom insisted she go to school. Since she was already going in late and would only be gone a few hours, Sadie decided not to pick this fight and went with her mom.

Sadie entered her class to quiet stares. Word was out about Lucky's disappearance, and Sadie thought her classmates probably thought she was a terrible horse owner for losing her horse. She broke the silence by announcing, "We have Lucky back now, and he's going to be fine."

Mr. Edwards led the class in a round of "Hip hip, hooray; hip hip, hooray; hip hip hooray," which embarrassed Sadie, but also made her laugh. And then Mr. Edwards said, "Patrick, don't you have something you'd like to present to Sadie?"

"Um.... Sadie.... um, on behalf of the school, we have a donation we'd like to.... um.... present for your.... um.... auction tomorrow." He and Allie went to the cloakroom and returned with a giant fake check that had $500 written on it. They presented it to Sadie.

Allie took over as the spokesperson because she seemed a bit more comfortable in the limelight. "Sadie, after your initial presentation we decided as a class that we wanted to do something to help, but we wanted it to be a surprise. Mrs. Hawkins helped our class organize a fundraiser. We made and decorated ten horse costumes, one for each of your horses, and we had students support and raise money for each horse from across the entire student body. We had a race in the gym, and called it the Preakness in honor of the famous horse race held annually here in Maryland as part of the Triple Crown series. It didn't matter who won, as long as they all crossed the finish line—which they did." That Allie McGlade was a chip off the old block.

Mr. Edwards stepped in. "So, from your supporters at the Willis School, congratulations on finding homes for all ten horses, and we hope our donation helps in some way."

Sadie was stunned with this unexpected gift. She now had the newfound support of hundreds of her peers, and her teachers, and Mrs. Hawkins. The confidence that had dwindled over past few days slowly started to come back. She would need it for her final challenge.

ᴥ20ᴥ

CAN THEY SAVE THE HORSES?

November 11th was Veterans Day, a day of remembrance for the nation's past and current armed forces veterans, and a day always honored in Sadie's family. This would be a Veterans Day like no other.

Grandma kindly volunteered to stay behind from the action to nurse Lucky back to health. Mom, Sadie, and Austin departed for the auction at 6:00 a.m., leaving plenty of time in case they got lost or ran into heavy traffic. They headed north toward the Hamilton Auction, and Sadie ran through her plan with the family again to ensure she had all bases covered.

Sadie wished she had a few more helpers, but was thankful for her team. A team as mighty as it was small. Her group included her mom, Austin, Jessi, Ms. Clarke, J.C the retired jockey, and herself. The addition of J.C. to the team had come as a surprise last night, and she was touched that such an important and respected person had volunteered his time to help her.

Sadie's major role was to bid on the horses as they came up for auction because she was the only one who could truly identify which horses she was determined to save. Mrs. Navarro would stay close by Sadie's side to step in if necessary or if people did not take Sadie seriously. She was also in charge of the finances, paying for each of the horses, and keeping track of the funds.

Austin would be the runner, alerting Sadie when one of her horses would come through the chute. He knew the horses' descriptions well after working so closely with Sadie. Austin had a way of looking like he fit in anywhere, so he could roam the aisles of the auction barn unobtrusively.

Jessi and Ms. Clarke would meet Sadie's family at the auction with the horse trailers, hay, water, halters, and lead ropes. Between Jessi, Ms. Clarke, and J.C., there would be enough people to watch the loaded horses and walk the newly purchased horses out to the trailers. Between the three of them were ninety years of combined horse experience, and Sadie knew she could rely on their expertise.

Everyone had cell phones, including Sadie, since Sergeant Lucero recovered hers during OPERATION RESCUE LUCKY. They had each others' numbers. Just to be safe, Sadie recorded the numbers on laminated cards and handed them out. She sure hoped they had cell phone coverage in Hamilton, because if not, Austin would be doing even more "running" than planned.

Before she knew it, they were there. The pictures and videos of the auction grounds that Sadie had seen on the internet did not begin to capture the enormity of the place. All kinds of people and horses were there, including a large number of Amish horse and buggy carriages in the parking lot.

Because it was still early, Mom parked and suggested they take a good look around. The doors were open and plenty of people were already at work. Austin took one look at Sadie and said, "Don't worry, you'll be fine. Remember Grandma's 'signs?'" He started to trace "I believe" in the air and smiled at Sadie. She couldn't help but smile back. Austin always had a way of knowing exactly when she needed faith.

The threesome walked through the large double doors and entered the auction house like they knew exactly what they were doing. The auction drew people of every age, from toddlers to old men. Warm inside, it smelled like a livestock barn, which had a slightly different, coarser odor than a horse barn. It was extremely noisy in the main hall and Sadie stared at what would soon become the main auction block.

Large bleachers lined each side of a rectangle pen. Some of the seating was already occupied, but the people looked to be eating and socializing, not planning their purchases. Bright lights shone in the pen, and Sadie saw the table around which the auctioneers would sit.

They decided that a spot in the left hand corner would be the best place for them to see, and make themselves visible to the auctioneers. Austin would also have easy access to them as he ran back and forth between the horses and the team members. They would need to come back before long to secure the spot.

Now the hard part – finding Sadie's horses. In all her imaginings, Sadie never pictured the auction being this big. Somehow she thought she would walk into the auction barn and find all her horses together, just as they were during the "encounter." That was not the case at all. They walked the rows and rows of animals looking for Sadie's horses. Every now and then, Austin would ask, "Is this one of them?" when he saw one that he thought fit one of the descriptions. Each time, Sadie shook her head.

They saw miniature horses, donkeys, and the largest draft horse any of them had ever seen. They saw chestnuts, pintos, bays, grays, ponies, horses, and even mules. Sadie was trying to keep a grip on herself, but as she looked into the appealing eyes of each animal, it broke her heart. She wanted to save them all.

However, at this point, she couldn't even find the horses she had promised to save, and they were at the end of the barn. For the first time in a long time, she started to have serious doubts.

What if the "encounter" never really happened? she thought. *What if I really just imagined it because I banged my head a few too many times training Lucky, or because I was dehydrated, or stressed out over the move, and Dad, and everything else? And now I have almost $12,000 dollars of other people's money, two trailers, three experienced horse people, Mom and Austin all here for what may have been a dream. Not to mention that the entire school is rooting for me, and I went on Capitol News. Oh my gosh, and Delegate Bragg, and all the other people that were expecting these horses....*

"SADIE!" Mom finally yelled.

"What.... uh, sorry, Mom, what were you saying? I got kind of lost in a train of thought."

"A train.... must have been a locomotive," said Mrs. Navarro. " I just talked to that man over there. He works here, and said there are several more barns of horses. We'd better get moving if we are going to find all of your clients before the auction starts. We also need to get an auction number so the auctioneer will be able to identify us. I explained to him that you and I will be bidding together, and he said that wasn't a problem, as long as we stay together and I sign all the paperwork."

Austin moved ahead to the second barn, and a few minutes later Sadie's phone rang. Good, they had cell phone coverage.

"Hey," said Austin, "I think I've found Lucy and Ricky."

Sure enough, when they caught up with him, he'd found the ponies. Sadie gave them each a pat and asked them to believe in her, and assured them that she would have them out of here and into a good home by the end of the day. It was probably her imagination, but she really thought they understood. Austin took down the numbers assigned to the ponies for the auction, and Sadie was relieved that at least two of her horses were here.

A few minutes later, Austin spotted Goliath and Thor. "Well," he said, "I figured those would be the easiest to find – the big ones and the little ones." He went off to find Sunny and Spot because he knew he could recognize them. "And yes," he said, "I'll tell them you're here to save them," and he rolled his eyes.

Time was getting short, and Sadie's cell phone rang again. It was J.C. He and Ms. Clarke were there with the trailer parked, and wanted to know if they could do anything. Sadie said, "Yes, you can help me find the two Thoroughbreds, and see if you can get Vixen's tattoo." Sadie knew that if anyone could spot her Thoroughbreds out of a crowd it would be those two. "Oh, and don't bother checking the first barn, because they aren't there. Thanks!"

Mom looked straight ahead at a horse being led in and said, "That has to be Chance." She was right. Mom loved Arabians. She had a fondness for their faces and eyes, so it was no surprise that she could pick Chance out of the crowd. She took down his number, and they both went over to give him a pat and let him know that he had a great future ahead of him. In typical Arabian nature, he scratched his head on Mom's shoulder and seemed to nod his approval.

Down to the last horse. Hardball, the horse sponsored by her dad's unit. Maybe they would re-name him "Hard to Find." Sadie decided to go ahead and embarrass herself and started to call his name. She walked down the center aisle calling "Hardball, here Hardball," which garnered a few odd stares. But, she watched the horses, and sure enough, a horse with large Tennessee Walking Horse ears turned and looked. It was Mr. Hard to Find. She joked with him about being so elusive and told him not to worry, they weren't sending him to Afghanistan to be with the unit. He would be going to a lovely farm in Calvert County to wait for his forever home.

While Mom took down Hardball's number and location, Sadie checked in with Austin, who had found Sunny and Spot tied side by side. Always the planner, he had decided to take another lap around the barns to remind himself where the horses were and to calculate how long it would take him to get from point A to point B. Sadie called J.C. and was happy to hear that they'd found the Thoroughbreds right away, called in Vixen's tattoo to the Breeders Association, and were waiting for a call back.

Dad would have asked for a "time hack," had he been there, which meant it was time to seriously get in gear. It was now 7:45 a.m., and the bidding started in fifteen minutes. Mom grabbed Sadie's hand and dragged her through the barn at a jog, breaking the universal rule of "no running in the barn." Sadie didn't stop her and just tried to keep up. They ran to the office and filled out the paperwork for their bidding number, then ran for the seats they had picked out an hour ago. Sadie let out a sigh when she saw that were already taken.

She looked more closely, and was relieved to see it was Mr. Edwards and Mrs. Hawkins! They had run into Austin on their way in and asked if there was anything they could do to help. Austin suggested they save the seats.

They asked if there was anything else they could do to help, and Mom passed them the laminated cards with the cell phone numbers and asked if they could just lend a hand where needed. The only immediate issue was that they had not seen Jessi. She wasn't supposed to be there until 8:00 a.m., but if they could locate her, that would be a great help. Most importantly, Mom thanked them for the moral support.

Before Mr. Edwards and Mrs. Hawkins left, Mr. Edwards pulled a bracelet out of his pocket and handed it to Sadie to bring her luck. He had made it himself when showing the kids how to make crafts for the upcoming Kenyan Market Day. It had multi-colored beads, stars, and running horses, and words that read, "I Believe." When Sadie asked him how he knew about Grandma's "signs," he said, "I didn't know about your grandma's signs, Sadie, although I'd like to hear about them later. I just know you believe in what you are doing. And I believe in you." With that, her teacher and librarian left.

Sadie looked over the list of auction numbers for

all her horses. This could get tricky because the horses were not in numerical order. Further, she was the only kid bidding on horses.

So many types of people were here – clean, not-so-clean, Western riders, English riders, farmers, professionals, and a few that just looked like horse traders. She wondered if she was the only rookie bidder.

The auction began, and the volume in the hall doubled immediately. Sadie had a very hard time understanding the auctioneer with the "abbidaya jabberida yyyyeaahh and do I hear $400? Abbiday jabberida yyyeahh..." *Yikes.*

Luckily she'd get to watch for awhile before her first horse came up. A young woman in a flashy Western riding outfit entered the pen, riding a gorgeous buckskin Quarter Horse and showcasing Western movements such as turn on the haunches and sliding stops. Sadie marveled at how she could move the horse so fast in such a small space, and how the horse didn't react at all to the crowd and the overbearing sound of the loud speakers. A few interested buyers continued to raise their bidding paddles until the auctioneer ended with, "annnnddd SOLD to number 346 for $1250."

It was fast-paced, but didn't look that hard, as long as she could understand the auctioneer. Sadie watched a few more sales and mentioned to her mom how surprised she was that the horses were so well behaved. An older woman behind Sadie leaned down and said in her ear, "That's because half of 'em are drugged." Sadie turned around to look at her to see if she was kidding, but she clearly wasn't.

Austin appeared at the corner to say, "Your first horse is coming up three horses from now. It's Sunny. I'll only know a few horses ahead of time." Since the chute where Austin stood wasn't that far away, he could easily let them know when one of Sadie's horses was coming up.

Sadie listened closely to decipher the auctioneer banter. There were two of them, one much easier to understand than the other. As Sunny approached the chute, with Austin pointing to her, Sadie listened to the harder-to-understand auctioneer describe her. He began the bidding at $500. Sadie didn't raise her paddle, but a beady-eyed man with a cowboy hat right across from her, number 122, did. Ouch, this one was going to cost. Prepared for battle, she heard "Do I have $550?"

She raised her paddle high, the auctioneer said something she couldn't understand, and a ripple of laughter went through the crowd. The number 122 bidder squinted at her, and the auctioneer asked for $600. Number 122 raised his paddle again, never taking his eyes off Sadie. Sadie stared right back and bid $650. The auctioneer continued his chatter, but no more paddles were raised. "And SOLD to number 235." Sadie had her first horse.

Sadie hadn't thought the bidding would be so confrontational. She realized that some other folks might be there for the same reason she was, to save horses. She knew some of them were not.

Austin told them it was going to be at least another twenty minutes before her next horse came out.

"Mom, I'd like to take a break if that's okay with you."

"That's fine," Mom said, "but I don't want you wandering around here alone. Stick with Austin; I'll save the seats."

She and Austin went outside for a breath of fresh air, and Sadie's phone rang. Jessi had arrived, and she'd parked right next to Ms. Clarke, which would make the loading much easier. Jessi and Ms. Clarke had met up with Mr. Edwards and Mrs. Hawkins, glad to have the extra hands. Jessi told Sadie that Ms. Clarke wanted to talk to her and put her on the phone.

"Sadie, you have to get Vixen." Ms. Clarke spoke with an urgency Sadie hadn't heard before. "DO NOT let anyone outbid you. She doesn't look too good right now, and she's going to be so scared that she'll be acting crazy. It shouldn't be hard to get her. But there's more to this story than I can get into right now. You've done a great thing, girl, and this horse is going to thank you. Look, I have to go now, but see you soon," ended Ms. Clarke.

Geez, as if the pressure wasn't high enough already. Sadie returned to the bleachers and whispered the updates to Mom.

The next horse in the chute was Thor. Bidding started at $500, with no takers. Down to $400, with no takers. Sadie thought he was fantastic and thought the other people were crazy, but she was not about to bid higher than necessary. The scar on his legs and his age probably made him unappealing, but he'd be perfect for someone. She got him for $225.

And so the day continued. As Sadie bid on her horses, she developed a following. The crowd cheered each time she won, and some people started ganging up on others who tried to outbid her. She had become a celebrity of sorts. Not everyone joined in with her, but she was not there to make anyone happy. She was there to save her horses.

One of the horse handlers rode Goliath into the

ring, and Sadie was amazed again by the horse's size. She swore his front leg was wider around than she was. The six-foot tall man riding Goliath appeared the size of a jockey. Goliath seemed confused by the rider, probably because his horse career had been pulling carriages, not hauling riders on his back. Goliath appeared proud with his head held high, oblivious to the fact he was filthy, ungroomed, and up for sale to complete strangers. Sadie had to save this proud soldier who looked like he'd spent a lifetime dutifully following orders.

"Addidda jabbidya draft horse jabbida yyyeahh, do I hear $200?"

Fortunately this time it was the slower auctioneer. Of course, it was like the slowest car in a NASCAR race, but better than having to try to decipher the super-fast talker. While she considered all this, she saw a paddle from across the room go up from an older spectacled-man with a determined look to him.

"Sooooo $200.....do I hear $250, $250 for this beast of a horse....abbida jabbidya," and Sadie raised her paddle high. Beast! Thank goodness Goliath didn't understand that.

Sadie surveyed the crowd while the auctioneer began his banter for the next bid request. She'd been so focused on the auction that she hadn't realized how many more people had entered the arena during the bidding over the past few hours. As she perused all the different faces, she tried to draw strength from the support in the crowd. As she looked around, she saw him again, number 122, who had tried to outbid her for Sunny. She caught his eye just as he raised his paddle. Not again. She also realized that the bidding was up to $350 now. She *had* to stay focused.

179

Staring at Goliath and listening intently to the auctioneer, she heard it loud and clear, "$400," and she stood up and raised her paddle. Goliath looked back at her, appeared to stand taller, and Sadie thought he might just be feeling good that someone wanted him. At this point, his rider almost did a circus trick. He put his weight on his hands, leaned forward, kicked back his legs and took the huge leap down from Goliath. This garnered applause and a few laughs from the audience. The rider had demonstrated that Goliath could be ridden, and his vaulting routine showed that the "beast" could handle interesting maneuvers on and around him without being fazed. Sadie wished they'd stop making Goliath look so good to other bidders!

Now the bid was $600. Sadie hadn't even had time to raise her paddle during the last few volleys. A small war erupted between number 122 and the older man who had first bid on Goliath. Obviously they knew each other, and Sadie sensed the tension all the way across the arena. She sat down, and jumped back up again attempting to get the auctioneer's attention, when she heard, "abbidya jabbera $700."

The auctioneer ignored her. Sadie looked pleadingly at her mom, who patted her leg and said, "Stick with it, we'll get there." But she didn't sound very convinced.

Sadie's mind raced. If she paid so much for Goliath, would she still be able to buy Vixen? She knew how much money she had left, and she really hadn't expected to spend this much on Goliath. She knew he was special, but she hadn't thought others would see it, too. And why was the auctioneer ignoring her? And even her crowd support seemed to have dwindled. She had to think fast.

"Mom, what if I half-lease Lucky to someone else at the barn for a few months? It could save a few hundred dollars that we could use right now. What do you think?"

It seemed to be getting noisier and noisier and that constant jabbering of the auctioneer in the background was almost more than Sadie could take. The horse handler continued to parade Goliath around the ring, and Goliath continued to march smartly. While waiting for her mom's answer, Sadie heard it: "SSOOOLLLDD to number 122 for $850."

Sadie jumped up and cried out, "No!" But her voice was drowned out by the noise and commotion. She watched Goliath depart the arena, and his head seemed to hang low.

"Sadie, I'm sorry. I don't know what to say," her mom said, sounding sorrowfully defeated.

~21~

LOST AND FOUND

The reality that she had lost Goliath was slowly sinking in. Sadie sat with her eyes glued to the ground, a look of disbelief on her face.

"Sadie," her mom said gently, "Vixen is about to come out."

Despite her despair about losing Goliath, Sadie knew she had to pull it together. At least she would save nine of the ten she had promised.

Sadie and Mom watched anxiously as Vixen came out. Vixen was led, not ridden. Her eyes were wide with fear, and she stepped in every which direction. Maybe it was sadness from losing Goliath, but Sadie's heart was breaking for Vixen. The auctioneer on the ground tried to look in her mouth to guess her age from her teeth or a tattoo, and she reared. "Forget it," he said, "She's going as is."

Sadie was the only bidder, and paid $35 for the

striking Thoroughbred filly. Luckily, this was far less exciting than the last bidding session. Sadie didn't know it, but Ms. Clarke had come in to watch, and was standing right behind her. She put her arms on her shoulders and said, "Good job."

Sadie turned around, pulled the horseshoe clip out of her hair and handed it to Ms. Clarke. "Thank you," she said, "We made a deal, and I won't need this anymore." *It won't help me save Goliath now,* she thought. *But at least it helped me save the others.*

Ms. Clarke hesitated for a moment, then took the hairclip with a smile.

The auction house erupted in applause. The clapping sounded different from before. This clapping was sheer admiration, showered on Sadie by the crowd. Feeling very odd, she turned to the people and gave a festive bow, and smiled and waved, wondering if they could see the tears in her eyes. The auctioneer said something she couldn't understand, and the next thing she knew almost everyone was standing and cheering. Her mom encouraged her to step down from the bleachers, and they left after turning around to wave to the crowd one more time.

Austin somehow avoided the moment of fame, but caught up with them as soon as they paid their final horse bill.

"I'm so sorry about Goliath," he said.

"Me too," and she looked at the ground. "I can't believe it. I just keep reminding myself about the others." She thought about his big, proud eyes and put her hands over her eyes as the tears came. Sometimes even famous Horse Savers couldn't save them all.

Sadie had stayed within budget and was going to be able to pay the gas bill for transporting the horses. The money she had left over, some of which had been intended for Goliath, would go into a fund for unexpected expenses during the next few months. Who knew, there were obviously many more horses that needed to be saved, and maybe Sadie could help again someday.

Once outside and away from the auction house, Ms. Clarke confided that Vixen had been stolen in Florida months ago. Nothing had come up during the computer searches because someone had changed her name along the way. They had run her tattoo against Thoroughbreds nationwide, not just in Maryland.

Over the past few months there had apparently been a good deal of press about Vixen's case, and the filly's owners were very distraught about her disappearance. Sadie remembered how frightened she had been over Lucky's disappearance and her heart went out to them. So, this was a Triple Crown win! Vixen was saved, the owners were overjoyed to find her, and TPR would only have to hold her until the owners arranged transportation back to Florida.

The Horse Saving team gathered at the two trailers to celebrate their success. Sadie didn't know what to think. She felt elated that they had saved nine horses. She felt sick when she thought about Goliath's fate.

In a heartfelt speech Mr. Edwards declared, "Look at the power we have, all of us coming together from many walks of life, to help these animals who could not speak for themselves. Led by Sadie, we changed the course of fate for the betterment of these horses' lives."

Although speeches really weren't Sadie's thing, and her emotions were whirling, she pulled it together and thanked everyone for their help. She publicly recognized her mom for all she had done and let everyone know how much help Austin had been. She thanked her new friends, Ms. Clarke and J.C., and her old friends Jessi, Mr. Edwards, and Mrs. Hawkins. She ended with, "And on behalf of Chance, Sunny, Hardball, Spot, Lucy and Ricky, Thor, Buster, Vixen, and...." She paused, choking back a tear, "Thank you for saving us."

"It's not your fault about Goliath, Sadie," Jessi said. "You did all you could, and you did a great thing today for nine horses." Everyone nodded in agreement.

"Thanks," Sadie said, feeling a lump in her throat. "It just doesn't seem fair."

The members of the team disbanded and walked toward their respective vehicles. Sadie turned and took one more look at the auction barns.

As they walked to the car, Sadie felt a tap on her shoulder and someone said, "Excuse me, could I have a moment of your time?" When she turned around, she came face to face with the number 122 bidder, who had won Goliath. She knew what she felt now, hatred.

He tipped his cowboy hat to Sadie and her mom. Sadie wanted to scream at him, *No, you jerk, don't you know what you did?!*

The man introduced himself as Eddy Carl, owner of Carlingsford Farms.

"Look, kid, I'm really sorry about the horse, and..."

"His name is Goliath," Sadie interrupted defiantly.

"Okay, I'm sorry about Goliath, but let me try to explain..."

"There's no explaining!" Sadie cut him off again, "I came here to save ten horses, and you ruined it! I already had a home for him, and..."

"Sadie!" Mom broke in. "Sadie, this man is trying to talk to you, and you're being terribly rude. I'm sorry, Mr. Carl, please continue," and Mom shot Sadie one of those *enough-out-of-you* looks.

"Thank you, ma'am. Sadie, if you'll please just give me a minute. You see, I understand. I'm not that different from you. I come here to the auction to pick up horses for my farm, but also to save a few. That fellow bidding against me? Zack Grimes. I happen to know for a fact that he's one of the 'meat buyers', meaning the only reason he's here is to buy horses to sell them in other countries for their meat. That's why he wanted Goliath. Because he's so big."

The thought nauseated Sadie. She had calmed down enough to listen to Mr. Carl, the first male Horse Saver she had ever met.

"I have a lot of experience doing this, so I know he stops bidding once the price has surpassed what the horse is worth on the meat market. I figured you didn't know that, and although you probably hate me right now, please try to understand that I am on your side. I came over here to tell you that I'll give you Goliath for whatever you want to donate to Carlingsford Farms. And if that's nothing, that's fine, too. I believe in what you are doing, and I'm happy to see a new generation of Horse Savers at work. I don't need Goliath. I just couldn't let Zack Grimes get him, and I wasn't sure you'd be able to."

Sadie couldn't believe it. This man, who she had detested moments ago, was actually on her side. Awkwardly, she reached out her small hand to shake his big, rough hand, and raised her head to meet his eyes. She took a deep breath. "I'm sorry, Mr. Carl. I didn't know. It's just that I didn't expect anyone else would be looking out for Goliath. Thank you for what you are doing, and what you did for us."

"Apology accepted, young lady. Ma'am," he turned to Sadie's mom, "you've been awful quiet."

"I'm sorry Mr. Carl, you're right," said Mrs. Navarro. "I'm just trying to figure out how much we can afford to donate to your farm. I think we can pay you the full price you paid, $850."

"Well thank you ma'am, let's consider it done."

Sadie felt relief wash over her. Suddenly she said, "Mom, can you please pay him on your own? I have to go tell Goliath what's going on! And I have to tell Jessi that she has one more horse to load!"

"Okay," Mrs. Navarro said, "But you and Austin go together. I'll let Jessi know right now so she doesn't leave. And I'll tell her to pass the good news to the rest of our team!"

Sadie barely waited for her mom's approval before she bolted in the direction of the barns to try and find Goliath, saying, "Thanks again Mr. Carl!" as she went.

They wound in and out of aisles of horses moving either towards the auction block or off to their new destinations.

"There he is!" Austin pointed to Goliath, lined up with a few horses, all destined for Carlingsford Farms. Goliath's head hung low. Sadie approached him with a soothing cluck.

"Hey, Goliath, it's me, Sadie." He raised his eyes, but not his head. He seemed so despondent. "Goliath, I have excellent news," she continued, as she got closer and reached over to stroke his massive neck. He turned his neck slightly, as if to say, "Go on...."

"Goliath, you're coming home with us, and you

are going to a home where you will be loved, and where you will help other people. I can tell that you are such a good soldier – or sailor, I'd prefer – and you will love your new job and will be great at what you do. People will take care of you, and look forward to seeing you, and you will be the best therapeutic riding horse ever. I know it!" She reached in and hugged his huge front leg, which she now confirmed was as big around as she was.

Goliath affectionately turned his head and nudged her, which would have knocked her over if Austin hadn't been there to catch her. "Thanks buddy," she said to Goliath. "Can you please pass on to your horse buddies here that they are lucky to be going to Carlingsford Farms? They are safe now." Sadie stood back, came to attention like her dad had taught her, and saluted the brave and proud Goliath. Beast – hah!

Sadie couldn't wait to get home to tell Lucky they had succeeded, but somehow she sensed he already knew.

Sadie and Austin returned to the parking lot to find that the team had re-grouped to celebrate the news about Goliath. There were high-fives all around. Before they went their separate ways, Mr. Edwards took some photos of the group and the horses, using Sadie's cell phone.

A single pair of hands started it, and a grassroots community finished it. All ten horses were saved, safe, and on their way to their new lives.

❦22❧

NEVER GIVE IN

The ride home seemed to fly by, and Sadie felt an overall sense of relief that she hadn't felt in months. Halfway home her phone rang. It was Grandma Collins saying she had a surprise for Sadie when she got to Loftmar. Sadie tried to pry the secret out of her, but there was no way. Grandma Collins loved suspense.

After Sadie and Jessi got Thor and Spot settled in one of Loftmar's fields, Sadie and Austin ran up to Grandma Collins to find out what the surprise was. Grandma pulled out her laptop and said, "You're going to be able to tell your dad about your day!"

Sadie, not meaning to seem ungrateful, didn't see what the big deal was. She e-mailed Dad all the time. Grandma knew this, so she was a bit confused. Grandma was busy typing on the laptop which she had set up on the picnic table outside the barn. The next thing she knew, she heard her dad's voice.

"See, this is called 'Skype,' and with it you can have a live video chat all the way to Afghanistan! Isn't that cool? I just found out how to do it, and Miss Jan was nice enough to let us use her wireless connection. I thought it would be great! What do you think?"

Sadie was unusually speechless. She stared into the screen to see her dad smiling, looking back at her in his desert camouflage uniform. He gave her the "thumbs up," waved, and said, "Don't you want to say hello? Or hola? Or something?"

Wow! It sounded like he was right there. Although she had tried to stay close to him through writing and a small number of phone calls, there was nothing like seeing him. Right away she felt how much she had missed his mannerisms, his voice, and his reassuring smile. She wanted to reach across the screen and squeeze him until he told her to stop, which she knew he would never do. Finally, she and Austin both blurted out, "Hi, Dad."

Mr. Navarro laughed. "Hi to both of you! Are you taking care of the house, Austin?"

Austin laughed. "You have no idea what it takes to keep this sister of mine in line."

Mr. Navarro laughed again. "Trust me, I think I do. You must have had quite an adventure. Tell me about it. Grandma hasn't told me anything, except that I needed to be at the computer at this precise time. You know how she is like that…" More laughter.

Sadie gave her dad a condensed version of the day, but made sure to include the highlights. She let him know that Hardball was on the way to his new home, and the entire unit would love him if they ever had a chance to meet him. She'd send pictures of him soon. Austin excused himself to give Sadie and Mr. Navarro some time alone, saying he would be back to talk to his dad in a minute.

"And Dad," Sadie continued, "you and Mom always taught me that things get done best as a team – just like you've always said our family is a team, and we all have our own strengths to contribute. The greatest team of people came together and saved ten horses."

"Yes, but they wouldn't have come together without you. You showed tremendous leadership, and I am so proud of you. You remember what Winston Churchill said: 'Never give in, never give in.' You never gave up. I don't think you realize how much courage it took to keep going when things were difficult. You celebrated small victories and then got right back to work. That's focus, sweetie, and there are grown people who still don't have as much focus as you've displayed in what you've done today. If I could, I'd pin a medal on you."

"Now you're embarrassing me, Dad. Hey, this is a laptop, and we can move. I want to show you Loftmar's new horse, Thor, and Sergeant Lucero's new police horse, Spot. Sergeant Lucero is coming here to pick him up tomorrow. He thought it would be less traumatic for both Thor and Spot to be together for an extra day before they got separated." She took a few steps away from the picnic table carrying the laptop with her back facing the pasture where Thor and Spot munched grass as if they'd been there for months.

"Can you guess which one is which?"

"Umm – let's see – the light colored one is Spot, and the spotted one is Thor?"

Dad, always the jokester. Sadie laughed and was relieved they were no longer talking about her.

"Oh, and here's Lucky," she said, as she panned the camera back to Lucky's stall. "See how well he's doing? What a trouper. Hard to believe he probably slept through all this today."

"He does look good, and even better in live video than in the pictures you've sent. You probably don't realize it because you see him every day, but he's grown and matured, Punkin, just like you."

Ugh, there it was again, the subject *back to her*. "Thanks, Dad. Hey, Austin's back, and Mom wants to talk too. Grandma said we could get bumped off this circuit at any time, so I want to make sure they have a chance to talk. I love you, Dad, and can't wait until you come home!"

"I'll be home before you know it. Te quiero, mi hija," Dad said in closing, telling his little girl he loved her.

Sadie smiled and turned away to let Austin in the screen before Dad could see her tears. Austin told Mr. Navarro about the events of the last three months from his perspective.

"You're doing a great job of running the house, Austin. Don't get too good at it, I'll be back before you know it!"

"Thanks, Dad," Austin said. "I love you. Mom wants to talk to you now."

"Okay, son, I love you too," said Mr. Navarro.

Sadie smiled as her mom stood in front of the laptop. Suddenly, she heard a loud noise in the background and turned back and mouthed to Mom, "What was that?"

"Hi, honey," Mrs. Navarro said, "great to see you. You look wonderful, as always. Hey, Sadie wants to know what that noise was."

"Oh, it's nothing. You know how these video computer things distort the sound. It must have sounded worse on that side than it did here."

"You're okay there, aren't you?" Mom asked.

"There's nothing to worry about, it's all normal."

Deciding to give Mr. and Mrs. Navarro some privacy, Austin went for a walk, and Sadie and Grandma Collins headed towards Lucky's stall.

Sadie and Grandma fussed over Lucky for a few minutes, and Grandma asked Sadie to point out Lucky's "sign." Sadie took Grandma's hand and traced over Lucky's "I Believe" markings, to Grandma's great delight.

"It's so obvious now!" she exclaimed. "Of course, I didn't have much time to dilly-dally around today looking for such things, since I had to focus on caring for Lucky. I refilled his water bucket four times and fed him an entire bag of carrots and apples. By then, I was his good friend, so he didn't mind when I gave him a bath. Good thing they have hot water here. He wouldn't have appreciated cold water in the November chill."

"I towel-dried him, which I guess they don't do anymore because he looked at me like I was crazy. As soon as he was completely dry, I let him out to go play with his horse friends for a little while. I remembered you said he loved that. I imagined him telling his friends about his ordeal. I know they all seemed happy to have him back."

Grandma probably could have gone on for another hour or so, but Mrs. Navarro came back.

"We got cut off, but not before we had a chance to talk. It was so good to see him." She handed Grandma back the closed laptop and said, "Thanks, Mom, for doing this for us. Now I see why you didn't put up a fight about staying home today. I know this wasn't easy to arrange in the barn! You really always are full of surprises. If you don't mind, I'm going to leave you two and go home now. I'm exhausted."

Sadie kissed her mom goodbye.

Sadie and Grandma turned their attention back to Lucky, Sadie still wondering about the noise she had heard.

"Thank you, Grandma, for taking such good care of Lucky today. I'm sure he knows you are the person who found him for me. Look at the way he looks at you. And I can't believe how much better he looks after just one day in your care! If he keeps healing at this rate, you'll even be able to see me ride him before you leave. Or maybe you can ride him?"

"We'll see, sweetheart, right now let's just give Lucky a big hug and make sure he understands that you've saved the horses. I think that will make him feel better more than anything. So Sadie stroked Lucky, talked softly to him, and showed him pictures of the horses on her cell phone. He nudged her and nickered, and then played with the phone with his nose.

"He knows, Grandma."

"How do you know for sure?"

"Watch. Lucky, how many horses do we have left to save?"

And they watched, while Lucky didn't tap the ground with his hoof at all.

"See? He understands!" reported Sadie with a big grin.

Grandma grinned back and they laughed together. It was a fun way to convince themselves that Lucky understood.

Then it was time to leave. After all, it had been a pretty extraordinary day for everyone.

"We did it, buddy," Sadie said to Lucky. She gave him a hug. There were soft tears in her eyes. "I couldn't have done any of this without you, Lucky. You got me through, and I know you're still here to get me through until Dad comes home." Lucky nickered softly and nuzzled the tears on her cheek.

That night, in the few moments Sadie lay awake in bed before falling asleep, she had time to reflect on these past few months. So many things had happened, and it was hard to think of them all. She wondered if she would ever again have such an eventful time in her life. Sadie helped her horses find a new purpose in their lives, and along the way she found a profound purpose in her own life.

She had moved to her sixth home.

Ten horses found ten new homes.

Everything happens for a reason.

Acknowledgements

I begin by thanking my wonderful husband, Jaime, for his positive support, encouragement, and persistent patience with me throughout the process of writing this book. He never questioned what I was doing; he believed in me. Everyone should be so lucky to have such strength in their lives.

My brother, Eddy, drew from his many years of teaching and creativity to help me enrich this book with learning, and make it educational as well as suspenseful. I thank my mom, Flo, for her support, her editorial guidance, and for listening to me throughout this venture.

I thank the organizations that allowed me to visit and research, to write realistic renditions of the events in this book. Freedom Hill Horse Rescue and Thoroughbred Placement and Rescue, Incorporated, opened their doors to me as they do to their horse clients. I was inspired by the dedication of the organizations' volunteers, who help improve the lives of horses in need. A large thanks goes to Loftmar Stables, for too many reasons to list here.

I thank Martha Rhoades-Spivey, MRS Photography, LLC, for her spectacular photos, and Jaime, again, for his photographic talent.

Finally, I thank my publisher, J.B. Max Publishing, for taking a chance on this unknown author, for making this book come to life, and for insisting on the pursuit of perfection in design and text.

About The Author

Valerie Ormond has spent the majority of her adult life as a Naval Intelligence Officer. The daughter of two English majors, and an English major herself, she always had a great interest in books and writing. Just prior to her retirement from the Navy, someone suggested she turn an idea she had into a book, and from there her second career began.

A lifelong horse enthusiast, Valerie enjoys bringing horses into the lives of people who may not otherwise have the opportunity. She is proud to have put over 100 people on horses for the first time, ranging in age from one to seventy- one.

Her education includes a Master of Strategic Studies from the U.S. Army War College in Carlisle, Penn.; a Master of Strategic Intelligence, Defense Intelligence College, Washington, D.C., and a dual Bachelor of Arts degree in English and Mass Communication from Towson University, Towson, Md.

She lives with her husband, Jaime Navarro, a career Naval officer, in Bowie, Maryland. They enjoy the company of family and friends, three horses (including "Color Me Lucky"), and two dogs.

Also Available from JB Max Publishing:

Jenny and Jason are going on an adventure. They have never ridden before, but that is about to change. With ever mounting excitement that they will soon be on the backs of their favorite horses, they learn about brushes, tack, safety rules, and that no two horses are alike.

The colorful and entertaining cast of characters guides Jenny, Jason, and the reader through the world of horses. Forty illustrations bring the book alive, and the element that is prominent throughout is the joy and bond that exists between horse and human.

Of course, no day at the barn is complete without a few unexpected events. Will Jenny be able to handle the spirited Amaretta? Will Jason overcome his pre-ride jitters?

Visit www.redridingbook.com to learn more.

Available from Veda Readers

Teacher's Tack for Believing In Horses provides educator lesson plans, discussion activities, and fun learning opportunities for a wide variety of ages and reading levels. This 78-page comprehensive guide will make any teacher's job easier.

www.believinginhorses.com/veda_readers